THE BLUE LINE DOWN

the Blue Line Down

MARIS LAWYER

HUB CITY PRESS
SPARTANBURG, SC

Copyright © 2021
Maris Lawyer

Book Design Lead: Kate McMullen
Cover photo: © Dave Herring / via Unsplash (front)
© Jonny Mckenna / via Unsplash (back)
Proofreaders: Jacque Lancaster, Harrison McGinnis

Library of Congress Cataloging-in-Publication Data

Names: Lawyer, Maris, author.
Title: The blue line down / Maris Lawyer.
Identifiers: LCCN 2021006396
ISBN 9781938235849 (paperback)
ISBN 9781938235856 (ebook)
Subjects: LCSH: Baldwin-Felts Detectives, Inc.—Fiction.
Coal mines and mining—Fiction.
GSAFD: Historical fiction.
Classification: LCC PS3612.A9568 B58 2021
DDC 813/.6—dc23
LC record available at https://lccn.loc.gov/2021006396

The South Carolina Novel Prize is funded by the South Carolina Arts Commission, Hub City Press,
and South Carolina Humanities. The South Carolina State Library is a founding partner.

Hub City Press gratefully acknowledges support from the National Endowment for the Arts,
the Amazon Literary Partnership, South Arts, and the South Carolina Arts Commission.

HUB CITY PRESS
200 Ezell Street
Spartanburg, SC 29306
1.864.577.9349

FOR BENJAMIN

THE BLUE LINE DOWN

Preface

Jude sat on the doorstep while Willis was being born. All he could hear was Ma inside screaming, and the other woman talking to her in a quiet voice. Pa was not home. He was still in the mines.

The screaming did not stop for hours. Jude sat on the doorstep during that time, the stillest he had ever been in his life. He watched the littlest children leave the schoolhouse and chase each other home, some starting up games of marbles in flat patches of dust. Most of the older children were in the mines and hadn't come out with the other men yet. Pa hadn't told Jude to come to the mines yet, and he sometimes wondered how many years he had left. Jude never went near the black maw of the mines, gaping like a raw bullet hole in the side of the mountain, where the men shambled in each dawn and shambled back out at dusk, filthy from head to toe.

Jude could hear Ma whimpering, followed by more cries of pain and the midwife shushing her. Jude began to wish he had not skipped school. He had never been so still in all his life.

The men came out of the mines past dark, and Jude saw Pa with his lantern making his way home. Jude took his chin out of his hands and sat up straighter. Ma was groaning in the house, and Pa heard it. He dropped his things and ran inside.

Jude rose to his feet and followed. The other woman helping Ma had her hand on Pa's chest, blocking him from the bedroom, speaking low and fast. Ma started screaming again. The woman turned and ran back in, and Pa followed. They did not close the door, and Jude approached the door slowly to look inside. Ma was laying on her side with her back to him, and she had one leg propped up on the footboard of the bed. Her white nightgown was wet and streaked with red around the bottom. Jude put both hands over his mouth, afraid they would hear his breathing.

It got quiet then. Ma's cries cut off, like when someone presses a hand against a guitar's strings to stop the sound. Pa's hand was on Ma's forehead, and the woman's hands were inside the nightgown. She pulled out a big, purple baby, and Willis broke the silence with his squalls.

Ma wasn't moving. Her head lay back stiff on the pillow, her eyes watching the ceiling. Jude could not move, could only look at her still, white face from across the room. Pa stroked Ma's forehead, his black hands leaving streaks of coal dust on Ma's skin. The midwife was putting Willis in a towel and came up to Pa.

"It's a boy, Hezekiah," the midwife said.

Pa did not reach out to hold the baby. He would not look at it.

An Irish girl started coming to the house. Her name was Linnet Myers and she was only nineteen years old, and looked even younger, but she was married and had a baby and was already pregnant with another. She nursed Willis and took care of him during the day when Jude was at school and Pa was in the mines.

Linnet Myers told Jude he could call her "ma'am," which made him wrinkle his nose, and she was always scolding him for snatching dried apples from the pantry or digging holes in the front yard looking for worms. Ma had rarely scolded Jude— if he stole a treat from the pantry, she'd utter a harmless fuss and ruffle his hair, shooing him on his way. Jude used to sit on the kitchen stool to watch Ma cook, but now he spent most of his afternoons leaning against the side of the woodpile, watching beetles crawl between the logs. On bad days, days when he didn't understand why Ma had died, he would find stones in the yard and hurl them at the yard crows. But he didn't mind Linnet Myers too much, because she took care of Willis as tenderly as her own baby. Linnet's little girl called her mother "ma'am" too—Jude found this ridiculous, until he realized it was the same word for mother. He kept calling Linnet Myers "Mam," but now he no longer minded.

Pa didn't pay any attention to Willis. Right after Ma died, Willis would raise Cain because he was wet, but Pa wouldn't do anything about it. But the crying would continue till finally Pa got up, his face red as dynamite, and Jude felt sure he'd hit Willis, or yank him up and fling him out the window. Jude would run forward and scoop Willis up, crying, "I'll change him! I'll change him!"

When Willis started growing teeth, Pa wouldn't come near him because of his wailing. At the end of the day, Mam Myers would beat on the locked door, yelling, "Hezekiah Washer, you take your boy in! I've got a husband and babe of my own. You take your boy in!"

Pa would stare at the fire, the flames reflected in his black eyes. Jude crossed the room and opened the door as quietly as he could. Tears shone in Mam Myers's eyes when she saw him. Even with her belly getting big with the second baby, she looked like a kid. She bent down and put Willis, whimpering, into his arms, and pressed her lips on Jude's forehead.

"I'm sorry," she whispered. "I've got a babe of my own."

Jude took Willis inside to his own room, away from Pa. He wet a clean rag in the water basin and gave it to Willis to suck on. Willis was a big, fat baby with cheeks round as baseballs and bumpy rolls of pudge all up and down his legs and arms. Jude always laughed when he looked at him, because he had never seen anyone so fat. Everyone was all bones and muscle at the mines. Jude pushed his finger into Willis's cheek, watching the flesh dimple, and he smiled. It was a sign of excess; a sign that somehow, Willis was getting what he needed.

Pa still didn't ask Jude to go to the mines. He knew they could use the money, even the paltry scrip given to the child laborers. Jude would watch the miners—some of them Jude's own age— climb up the hill in the thin pink morning light, and he'd see them disappear into the mouth of the mine. Jude wondered if Pa kept him in school because he would be able to take care of Willis at the end of the day. Pa didn't like being beholden to the

Myers. Or, maybe he didn't want Jude in the mines. Sometimes Pa would go into long tirades about the way the miners were treated with the owners never setting foot below ground.

Willis began walking and talking, and he wasn't so dependent on Mam Myers, and some of the old widows in the mine camp helped watch him during the day. Jude didn't feel so nervous now that Willis could do more things for himself. He didn't need to be fed or changed, just looked after. But sometimes instead of staying home after school to look after Willis, Jude joined the other children playing games or setting pranks on the mine owner, Mr. Wagner. He lived off in Bluefield, but he had a nice house near camp that he sometimes stayed in when he wanted to look in on the miners. Jude and the other boys would stow wasp nests in the rafters or sneak snakes through the windows when they knew he was coming. They would laugh and laugh when they heard the commotion from Mr. Wagner. It was even better if Mrs. Wagner was with him, because she'd run screaming from the house.

Jude grinned ear to ear as he walked home after the pranks. Over the years he heard the other men grumbling along with his father about Mr. Wagner and his foremen, complaining about wages and hours and company scrip. Jude thought of the coal-black faces of the miners, his friends, and his pa whenever he set pranks on Mr. Wagner. It made it easier to shrug off the resentful glares of his peers as they passed the school up to the mines each day.

But one night, coming in late from a prank, Jude caught Pa giving Willis a beating. They were in Pa's room, and Pa was thrashing Willis's bare back with his belt. He held the belt on the leather end so that the buckle bit into Willis's fresh pink skin, drawing blood and leaving hard blue knots. Willis was screaming and struggling, but Pa kept pulling him back without saying a word.

Jude pressed against the doorframe, his heart beating so fast that he felt his head grow light. Pa had never beaten him before. He didn't understand why he was beating Willis now. He gripped the handle, ready to rush in, but a cry from Willis struck fear in his gut. What had Willis done to make Pa beat him? Jude had done plenty to make Pa mad, and all he had ever received as punishment was a tongue-lashing.

More screaming sobs, quieting into whimpers. Jude stayed where he was.

Willis started going to school before long. Mam Myers teared up on the day Willis went with Jude to the dingy schoolhouse, but Jude felt a deep sense of relief. If he was at school, Jude could keep a close eye on Willis. Jude didn't go out with the other boys to play pranks on Mr. Wagner anymore. He stayed home and tried not to let Willis out of his sight. But he could not keep Willis glued to his side, and sometimes he would come back after running to the company store and find Willis with a boxed ear. Jude did not let on that he knew about the beatings. He did not know how.

Jude went to Mam Myers after these incidents. Jude guessed that Mam Myers was catching on about Pa. She said very little whenever Jude stormed in, eyes hot with tears, holding Willis's hand. She would give Willis a bit of dried apple to eat and kiss the top of his head, her brows furrowed with something that looked like anger. When she stood back up though, the expression was gone and she would get Jude to help with dinner while Willis played quietly with little Florrie and the new baby.

"Peel those potatoes," Mam Myers told Jude.

Jude sat on an overturned bucket and hewed at the potatoes with a paring knife, head bent low to mask his anger and the hot tears mounting over his eyelids. He flicked the knife too hard and too fast, and sliced a long cut into his palm. Jude dropped the potato and knife with a cry and clutched his hand, relieved to let the tears come freely now. Mam Myers came over.

"Peeling potatoes is a chore for a calm mind," she said, rinsing Jude's hand and wrapping it in clean linen. "You get back to that bucket and cut those taters slow."

Hand throbbing, Jude obeyed and sat back down on the bucket. He lifted the knife and concentrated on grazing the blade carefully across the potato so that the skin curled off slowly and neatly. The tears stopped and his anger subsided into a cold, dull ache.

Willis grew into a fine-sized boy, shooting up four inches the summer that Jude turned thirteen. He never quite lost his fatness, but he shed the baby look in his face and turned into a big boy. Jude thought this might keep Pa from beating him, seeing as how Willis was big enough to put up more of a struggle. But nothing changed. Pa started drinking more, and sometimes he came home barely able to hold himself upright. He would hurl hateful words at his two sons, though he still never laid a hand on Jude. Willis did not cry anymore, or go to Mam Myers's for a slice of dried apple. Jude would find him crumpled by the woodpile behind the house, clutching his side with one hand.

"What's got you sitting back here?" Jude would ask when he found him.

"Just a quiet spot," Willis would answer.

His words came out in soft huffs, wincing to talk and breathe. Jude wondered if a rib was cracked, or even broken. Bile rose in Jude's throat as his rage mounted; he almost spoke, but something in Willis's face stopped him. His eyes were blank and dry, staring forward as if feeling nothing.

He would find Pa and make him pay. Jude stormed into the cabin, but Pa was not there. He moved on, his brain jumping like a hot kettle of boiling water. Jude roamed the camp, dark though it was, till he finally found Pa in the schoolhouse with the other men. There were no lanterns lit in the schoolhouse, and the men all sat in the chairs listening to one big man talk at the front.

"...come together, and there's nothing they can do but listen to you. Haven't you been trampled down long enough? Held under the thumb of slave drivers like Wagner long enough? It's time to rally, it's time—"

The man stopped abruptly, and everyone turned as Jude entered to schoolhouse.

"Hezekiah," one said sharply.

Pa looked at Jude with his hard eyes. "Git," was all he said.

"No," Jude said.

"Get him out of here," one man insisted.

Pa rose with a scrape of his chair and marched to the back of the room, seizing Jude by the arm and pulling him roughly out of the schoolhouse. When they had passed through the door, Pa flung Jude forward so that he nearly fell to the ground.

"Don't never disobey me," Pa said.

Jude straightened himself and faced his pa. "Why were they sitting all in the dark?"

"Ain't none of your business."

"I can make it my business if I want to," Jude said, and charged forward to push past Pa into the schoolhouse.

Pa seized him by the shoulders and flung him backward, turning red in the face, and Jude fell into the dust.

"You cross me again, boy, and—"

"Beat me," Jude spat, his blood boiling as he lifted himself off the ground. He rose to his full height and came up to Pa so that they were nearly nose-to-nose. He had grown about as tall as Pa, a fact neither of them had realized till now. "Beat me like you beat Willis."

Pa said nothing, and Jude saw a deadness in his eyes that he had never noticed before. How could he feel nothing, with Willis hiding behind the house with a cracked rib? Jude thrust his palms against Pa's chest so that he stumbled backward a few steps. A black look came over Pa's face then, and a trickle of fear broke through Jude's rush of courage. He spoke up again to distract from his fear.

"Why do you only beat Willis? What's he ever done to you?"

"You better shut up."

"It ain't his fault Ma died," Jude shouted. "It's just what happened. He didn't have nothing to do about it."

"I swear to God," Pa said. "I swear to God—"

With a movement swifter than Jude could have imagined, Pa pulled back his arm and struck him so hard that, for an instant, everything went black as Jude hit the ground. He regained a blurry consciousness a few seconds later, and Pa stood a couple feet away.

"See that you mind your lesson, son," Pa said, rubbing his fist anxiously with his other hand. "Don't speak to your Pa like that again."

Jude wiped his mouth and rose slowly. His entire head felt like a cracked egg. "You'll pay for it," he said. "Just see if you don't."

It didn't take much for Jude to figure out that the miners meeting in the dark schoolhouse wanted to unionize. The camp talked about it more than they should have. The big man at the front was a union man from the city and was working to organize the miners. They met only at night and did not gather at the schoolhouse again, but instead met in the miners' houses or in different locations. It kept Pa out of the house in the evenings, which Jude wanted, but he knew trouble was brewing.

He and Pa no longer spoke at all. Willis asked about it once, but Jude never explained to him what happened. An enormous bruise developed on the side of Jude's head where Pa had punched him, though most of it was covered with his hair. Only a little streak of maroon was visible on the side of his face, and this Jude took no pains to cover. He only wished that more of the bruise were visible. For the moment, it did not matter to him that Pa had walked away unscathed; the only thought that stuck in Jude's brain was that he had fought.

This satisfaction was snuffed the day that Willis turned ten. Jude had done odd jobs around the mine camp for months in order to afford a little pocketknife from the camp store to give to Willis as a gift, and Mam Myers had even made a layer cake. As Jude walked home from the store, he heard a commotion from within the cabin that made his heart stop. He flung open the door and ran inside and found Willis on the floor, his arms bloodied and his shirt torn, with Pa standing over him with the belt. He whipped him brutally, the buckle biting into Willis's chest, neck, and face, drawing blood that smeared over the floor.

"You fat—miserable—grub!" Pa was shouting. "If you had never been born—!"

Jude lunged forward, seizing Pa's arms. Pa turned and Jude caught a crazed look in his eyes he had never seen before. His breath reeked of alcohol.

"Let go of me!" Pa growled.

Jude looked at Willis on the floor. He was cut all over, his face blotched with bruises and one eyelid split in the corner and streaming blood. Willis looked up at him, his mouth opening and closing like a fish's.

Willis stumbled to his feet and ran out the door. Jude let go of Pa and rushed after him, calling his name. Willis ran blindly, and was far quicker than Jude would have thought possible. He called after him again and again. Jude did not immediately realize where they were running to till he saw Willis pause before the opening of the mine.

"Stop!" Jude yelled. "Willis!"

Without turning, Willis ran inside, and Jude rushed forward to the opening of the mine. He knew better than to go inside; all the miners had finished working for the day, and there were no lights anywhere. Jude called after Willis, pleading with him to come back out, but he never reappeared. Jude ran back down to the miner's camp and beat on the door of the nearest cabin. When Jude climbed back up to the mine, he had four or five miners following him, donning their lighted helmets and saying nothing. They did not ask any questions, only entered grimly into the mine.

The search continued till morning. Mam Myers sat with Jude during the early hours of the morning, handing him a potato and paring knife to keep his hands busy. Pa never came.

Just at dawn, a miner reemerged and approached Mam Myers and Jude.

"He's fallen into a gas pocket," the miner said. "We're getting him out now."

Mam Myers's hand flew to her mouth with a broken sob. Jude saw movement at the mouth of the mine as the other men surged forward, and he bolted. He knew better than to stick around.

He would kill Pa. He didn't know how, but he would kill him.

When Jude entered the cabin, he found Pa slouched in the chair, unconscious. The belt, with bits of skin still stuck to the buckle, laid on the floor like a snakeskin. Jude picked it up by its leather end and stood over Pa. He tensed his arm to lift the belt, to thrash the man to ribbons, but instead of lifting, his arm began to shake. Soon, he was quaking all over.

Jude went to his knees, wracked with sobs. He had never wanted to do something as badly as he wanted to make Pa pay for beating Willis. He couldn't get Willis's face out of his mind. The blood on his face, that look in his eyes. His hands shook uncontrollably; he dropped the belt.

Jude staggered away from the cabin. Dashing tears from his face, he marched away from the camp toward Mr. Wagner's house on the side of the mountain. A few candles were lit in the windows, and Jude pounded on the door. All traces of grief were gone from his face, replaced with a stony hardness that, had Jude been given a mirror, he would have found closely resembled his father's.

Mr. Wagner himself opened the door, wrapped in a dressing robe.

"Yes? What is it?" he asked, lifting a coffee cup to his mouth.

"The miners are trying to unionize," Jude said.

The coffee cup slowly lowered from Mr. Wagner's lips. "What?" he asked. "Why are you telling me this?"

"Hezekiah Washer's in charge," Jude said, then turned and walked off the porch.

Jude did not return home. He went instead to the Myerses' cabin, finding Mam Myers curled close to the hearth with her two daughters clutched tight to her side. Her young husband stood at the other side of the room, minding the kettle soberly. Willis's birthday cake waited on the table.

Mam Myers glanced up, her thin face glazed with tears. "Jude," she said.

Jude went to the little girls' room since it was empty. He shut the door behind him and sat against the wall, closing his eyes. Mam Myers stepped into the room before long, murmuring something to the girls about helping their father. She came and crouched before Jude, stroking the top of his head with her fingertips.

"I've laid Willis out in the other room," she whispered.

Jude's stomach turned.

"Are you hungry?" Mam Myers asked.

"No."

"I've got some pears in syrup," she said.

She did not offer the cake.

"No," Jude said again.

She was quiet for a moment. "Has anyone told your pa?"

Jude did not answer. A part of him wanted to be a very little boy and lean into Mam Myers's side, letting the frozen hurt thaw and pour out of him. But a larger part—a heavier part—would not allow him.

"Where did you run off to, then?" Mam Myers asked.

Jude drew his legs up to his chest and crossed his arms so that they rested on top of his knees. Mam Myers's fingers on top of his head stalled for a moment.

"Jude? Where did you go?"

"You'll see soon enough," Jude answered, welling up with sudden dread as he thought of Mam Myers and the little girls, and even quiet Mr. Myers who was always gone up to the mines. He had not thought of them when he was at Mr. Wagner's.

"Oh, lamb," Mam Myers sighed. "What have you done?"

Chapter One

Quarry Hill, Virginia, 1922

At least there was no uniform. On occasion Jude would notice Bradshaw don portions of his old army garb, but even he had no formal uniform as a Baldwin-Felts agent. Always, though, Bradshaw kept his shirt tucked tight into his trousers, his old military boots buffed till they gleamed. From his thickly muscled neck to his clean-shaven face, Bradshaw never shed his identity as an army lieutenant even in his role as a Baldwin-Felts brute: a stark contrast to Jude, who at twenty-four was leanly built and had three days' worth of stubble on his face.

Jude had not particularly wanted the promotion to Bradshaw's second in command. Regardless, the other agents followed him up the mountain with no objections, though several, like

Bradshaw, were former military men: older, bigger, and more experienced than Jude. More so than the ex-military, Jude was watchful of the ex-convicts. The Baldwin-Felts were not picky about their recruits. Two or three of the men with Jude had appeared in the papers mere months before, typically with the words "Robbery" or "Attempted Murder" printed over their photograph. With the rise of unionizing miners, however, the Baldwin-Felts were not above negotiating with the jailhouses for convicts who were eager for freedom and more than a little comfortable with physical confrontation.

There were few, if any, reasons for the other agents to follow Jude as a leader, at least in Jude's eyes. The only factor working in his favor were the rumors surrounding him, and Jude saw no reason to lay them to rest. On a couple occasions, he heard the other agents retelling Jude's story to the new recruits, embellishing on how Jude ("just a kid—not a whisker on his face") had turned over his entire mine camp ("after slitting his daddy's throat first") to the Baldwin-Felts, standing on the mountainside ("watching the whole place burn, like the devil himself"). The recruits would scoff, exchanging glances with incredulous grins and sneaking glances across the room at Jude, who was perpetually leaning against something—walls, furniture, whatever was nearby—resembling a lazy tomcat more than a clawing tiger.

Jude let them tell their version. He wasn't about to share his own. When he had first joined the Baldwin-Felts, just a kid in his teens, the rumors had felt like a knife in the gut. He relived that day when Willis was killed in the mines, and then, a few days later, when Mr. Wagner had summoned the Baldwin-Felts. It was an outbreak of brutality: the unionizers were routed out and beaten in their homes, in front of their own families. The men that fought back were clubbed to death, or shot. The men who didn't resist were abused almost as badly before being told to leave the county, with the understanding that reentry would have them shot on the spot. Jude had watched all this from the Wagners' front porch. He remembered Mr. Wagner sidling up beside him, clapping a hand on his shoulder.

"You did right, son," he had said.

Whether Pa had been killed, banished, or left for dead, Jude never found out, and it wasn't a matter that kept him up at night. The only conviction that, even eleven years later, tormented Jude was wondering if Mam Myers and her family escaped. He had hinted to her that the Baldwin-Felts were coming, though whether or not they had fled in time he never discovered.

After the Baldwin-Felts raid, the Wagners took Jude back to their home in Bluefield. The Wagners' daughter, Dorothy, had taken a shine to him and begged her daddy to keep Jude with them, which was how Jude came to work for the family, mostly as an errand boy and yard keeper. Dorothy was a year or two younger than him and followed him around incessantly; Jude tried to shake her, unconcerned with staying on her good side. He only wanted to be left alone.

Jude came to crave rigorous labor that pulled his mind away from Willis's death and the Myers family, preferring to focus on his own screaming muscles or the blisters pebbled over his palms. After turning seventeen, Jude was called into Mr. Wagner's office and met Bradshaw for the first time. There, he had been offered a job with the Baldwin-Felts.

"Mr. Wagner here's told me your story," Bradshaw had said, the corner of his lip lifting ever so slightly. "We take on men like you."

Jude set the other men to pitching camp in a clearing they came across, rubbing his palms together to warm his stiff hands. Here in the Virginian mountains, though a few wildflowers broke through the soil and the trees were beginning to bud, it was still bitingly cold in the middle of March. Jude felt his stomach growl and made orders to have a fire set up. He watched the men as they worked: the ex-military men, as expected, were quick to clear the campground of underbrush and had soon collected firewood to set into the center. The other men pulled their bedrolls out of their packs and were already claiming spots around the fire pit.

With a frown, Jude noticed Johnny Prince, one of the ex-convicts, already sprawled atop his bedroll with his hands under his head. Jude said nothing, knowing he would not last long there; sure enough, one of the ex-military agents kicked Prince's legs and told him to get up. Prince grinned and lazily raised himself.

Jude tried to recall what had gotten Prince into prison in the first place; he thought he remembered Bradshaw mention his crime in passing: assault, alleged rape, some act of violence. Jude's immediate impression of Prince had been of a mad dog, and he had never shaken that image. His clothes—not unlike Jude's—were always rumpled, often stained, and he didn't bother much with hygiene. Prince's hair was dark and fell in long, tight ringlets, which he kept combed through with oily brilliantine. His teeth all came to a canine point and were horrendously crooked, giving his smile a feral look.

Jude's thoughts turned when a fire began to lick up the pile of logs in the center of camp. He approached the fire, spreading his hands out to warm. The other men did the same, crowded around tightly. For a few minutes, they said nothing. Jude's eyes fell on the newest recruit, a kid named Harvey Morgan, who he was supposed to be training. Harvey couldn't be older than eighteen or nineteen, but he was solid and strong—came from a farm, Bradshaw had said, and Jude believed it. He was exactly the kind of kid you'd expect to find pitching hay or cleaning horseshoes.

"So when do we meet up with old Bradshaw?" Prince asked, breaking the silence.

Jude wanted nothing more than to unfold his bedroll and stretch out for the rest of the afternoon, but he knew that Bradshaw was waiting to hear that they had arrived.

"I'll be going up to the camp," Jude said, rubbing his hands in an effort to seal in the warmth. His eyes fell again on Harvey, and with a flicker of annoyance he gestured at the boy. "You—come on."

Saying nothing, Harvey stepped away from the fire and picked a couple of items from his pack to stuff into his pockets. Jude strode off into the woods, not looking to see if his trainee followed.

"Don't wander off," Jude called over his shoulder to the men.

The Baldwin-Felts were supposed to camp out before raiding the Plummer Mine in the morning. Bradshaw was already up at the mine and had been there for several weeks along with a handful of other agents. The mine manager had called them a month ago after catching word about his men trying to unionize.

The Baldwin-Felts prowled the camp throughout the day and night to try and catch the miners meeting. Bradshaw had ordered reinforcement from the Baldwin-Felts headquarters in Bluefield last week when he and his men sniffed out that the unionizing party was larger than they had initially believed. Now Jude and his group of agents were supposed to join Bradshaw and his men, with the orders to set up camp on the mountain away from the mine camp to keep their movements inconspicuous.

Jude hiked up the hillside, eventually hearing Harvey's heavy march following behind. Jude had no map and didn't even carry a compass; the sun was halfway across the sky, and that guided him well enough. He had a decent sense of direction, and was somewhat familiar with this mine camp anyway, as it was not far from the mine camp where he had been raised. It seemed that all the mine camps were dotted along the ragged blue line of the Appalachian Mountains, and you could almost count them like a string of pearls. On clear days, Jude would be able to see smoke rising on the other side of the mountain range, presumably where these miners worked and lived.

"How far away is this camp?" Harvey asked from behind.

"No more than a mile," Jude answered. He turned to look at Harvey, who was keeping good pace with him. Like the other agents, he had a revolver belted to his side, and it slapped him on the side of his leg as he walked.

"Ever shot one of those?" Jude asked, breaking off a protruding twig as he continued to climb up the mountain.

"Sure I have."

"At a man?" Jude turned again to see Harvey's face at this question. The boy's stride stalled for half a second, but only just. His young face was solemn when he replied, "No, can't say I have."

"That'll have to change soon enough."

"Are all raids—" Harvey began to ask.

"No," Jude interrupted. "It's not always a bloodbath. But if you're working under Bradshaw, you better be ready to use your gun."

"He's violent," Harvey said, his words posed halfway between a statement and a question.

The ground grew more steep, and Jude's breath grew labored—a reminder that he hadn't kept up much physical training as he lazed around the office in Bluefield for the past few weeks. "You could say he has a reputation," Jude answered, panting. "Ever hear about that trouble in Colorado?"

"Something about it," Harvey responded.

"They sent us out West for a while," Jude said. "Hired by Northern Coal and Coke. Lots of unionizing going on. Bradshaw was one of the elite they sent out. They killed thousands out there—come to think of it, I think that's how Bradshaw got promoted."

He recalled again his first meeting with Bradshaw, nearly seven years ago now. Bradshaw had been younger, sleeker, and loaded with the aggressive swagger of a man who had slaughtered dozens and been rewarded for it.

"Yeah," Harvey said. "I remember my pop spitting nails about it. But I was just a kid when it happened."

"Your old man can't be too happy about you being here, then."

Harvey said nothing for a few seconds. "He'll be grateful when I start sending money back," he said at last.

"Didn't want to try the army?"

"Ma wouldn't let me."

"You always do what your ma says?"

"No," Harvey answered. "My brother was killed in the War.

Didn't want to do that to Ma again. So I came here. Seemed like the closest thing."

Jude licked his lips, parched from the cold. "I didn't mean to—"

Harvey shrugged. "It don't stick with me like it used to."

Jude thrust aside a fir branch that barred his way. "Yeah," he said. "Good for you."

As they crested the hill, the mine suddenly opened out before them. Jude paused, surveying the landscape below, and the sudden treeless expanse stunned him at first, as if he had stumbled upon nakedness. The mine camp he had grown up in had at least maintained the semblance of a community, with a few hardwoods kept around the housing areas and the grass springing green, if a little unkempt, between the cabins. Here, without the furry spruce and cypress or even the bare trunks of the deciduous trees, the land seemed bald and ravaged. About a mile away Jude could see the mines dotted against a colorless face of rock, the outcrop of which looked like gray backs bent over.

"What a place to live," Harvey said.

"You get used to it," Jude said, moving on down the hill.

With the trees stripped from the surrounding land, it did not take long for Jude and Harvey to descend the hill and enter the camp. The acrid smell of coal and smoke permeated the camp, and coal dust darkened the sheet metal and split logs that made up the ramshackle huts. The men were all up in the mine still, and would not come out till after dark. Their wives and children milled about the camp. Women stood in the doorways of the cabins, and Jude recognized the reediness of their bodies—the sinewy arms, the angular faces, the network of their ribcages visible through the backs of their thin cotton shirts. Most of them were surely in their twenties and thirties, but they already wore the grim, weathered look of old women. Grubby children grasped at skirt hems or whined to be picked up.

Jude dropped his eyes. He thought of Mam Myers's two little girls, realizing that they must be young women by now. They had been Willis's playmates more than his, but in the old days they would bring him trinkets: feathers they found on the ground, or the odd violet that would manage to sprout in early spring.

Ahead, Jude could spot the company store, the only decent-looking building in the camp. It looked freshly painted, and in the window display were various luxuries: china egg cups, soft dolls with porcelain heads, brass pocket watches, and a few bolts of cloth and lace. These items would likely have never left the window, as the miners could rarely afford such things on their wages. Jude knew from experience that a little sack of corn meal and a corner of fatback were the things most likely to ever leave that store.

Baldwin-Felts agents lazed around the porch of the company store, some sunning themselves on the steps, trying to absorb warmth from the weak March sunshine. One or two were standing, their eyes trained on the nearby camp. Bradshaw was among them.

"Decided to arrive after all," Bradshaw said as Jude and Harvey approached. He had a darkly tanned face with long crow's feet around his eyes, which looked like bright blue crystals imbedded in clay. Bradshaw was a massive man, barrel-chested, with thick, powerful legs. He stood alert, focusing on the mine camp. "We've got to move fast on this one, Washer," he said to Jude. "They know something's coming."

Bradshaw turned away from the camp, acknowledging Harvey

with a brief, stony glance. He snapped his fingers and one of the agents stepped forward. "Where's that list?" Bradshaw asked.

Wordlessly, the agent turned and dug into a bag that sat slumping against the side of the store. He withdrew a folded piece of paper and handed it to Bradshaw, whose eyes darted over it quickly, grunting to himself.

"Here," he said, thrusting the paper at Jude. "That's who we take care of. Tomorrow."

Jude unfolded the list. Names covered the entirety of the paper, scrawled crudely in pencil. Jude looked up.

"Who do we exclude?" he asked.

Bradshaw scratched under his chin. "Seems to be only about two or three families not interested in unionizing, but we can't know for sure. So no exclusions."

"What if they're innocent?"

Jude and Bradshaw turned to look at Harvey, who had spoken up from the base of the steps. Bradshaw took the paper back from Jude and folded it deliberately. He came down the steps and stood before Harvey till only a few inches separated the two. Bradshaw pushed the piece of paper into Harvey's hand.

"They'll learn a lesson early, then, won't they?" Bradshaw said.

Chapter Two

The morning sunlight was weak after filtering through the treetops, and the men had difficulty rising. Despite this, Jude woke early. He should have rekindled the fire as soon as he woke, but he couldn't persuade himself to abandon the feeble warmth trapped inside his sleeping roll. Jude kept his half-numb hands busy by using his pocketknife to carve a broken-off branch he picked up the day before. It was the same pocketknife he had bought for Willis's tenth birthday—a simple blade, not particularly well made. No skill was involved at this stage of the carving, only the blunt paring of excess wood that left a scattering of chips in Jude's lap.

Jude fished out a flask from his pocket and tossed back a mouthful, enjoying the warmth of alcohol as it surged through him. He had taken up drinking around the same time he joined the Baldwin-Felts. He had tasted liquor before then, of course, but it was only after becoming an agent that he formed a real drinking habit. At first, Jude had drunk so the other Baldwin-Felts wouldn't think him unmanly; soon, however, he found the dulling sensation to be a constant temptation. It deadened his fear before a raid and made him forget unwanted memories. Jude took another swig, then fumbled with the cap when he noticed Harvey sitting up in his own bedroll, watching him.

"Best damn cola you'll ever put in your mouth," Jude said quickly. He wasn't particularly nervous about Harvey, but Jude had learned the hard way to be more careful about his drinking habit. A few months ago, he was nearly arrested for violating Prohibition; Bradshaw had bullied Jude out of trouble, but only just. Among the Baldwin-Felts, however, Jude had little to worry about, as most of them followed the same practice. He tossed the flask to Harvey, who barely caught it. "Have a taste, kid."

Harvey eyed the flask, then looked at Jude. "That's a funny way to drink cola, if you ask me."

"Tastes better in steel. I like it flat, too. Can't stand the bubbles."

Harvey tossed the flask back to Jude without opening it. "You got something you need me to work on, Mr. Washer?"

Jude winced. "Look, kid, I can't stand that. Save the 'misters' for Bradshaw, but keep me out of it. Name is Jude."

The other men were beginning to stir, and Jude crawled out of his bedroll. He shook the wood chips off the top of his bedroll and pocketed the roughly hewn block and the knife.

"Up and at úem," he said loudly. "Bradshaw's waiting."

The other agents rose, packing up camp. Out of all the men,

Johnny Prince was the only one who moved vigorously. He had a grin stretched across his entire face.

The plan was to meet Bradshaw on the way up to the camp in order to distribute the guns and divide the men into teams. Jude tried not to think of Bradshaw's command to hunt down all the miners without discrimination; he focused instead on leading the men up the hillside, watching his own breath rise in white clouds through the cold air.

The sun had not fully risen by the time Bradshaw and his men came murkily into view. They looked like blue silhouettes in the dim light, the flare of a cigarette butt occasionally blooming in the dark.

"Distribute the guns," Bradshaw said, skipping a greeting as usual and moving toward the men. "We've lost enough time already."

The men with Bradshaw reached around themselves and pulled forward awkward bundles. They began to draw out Springfield rifles and distributed bullets for the revolvers that they all carried already.

"We are preparing to confront the unionizers in the Plummer Coal Mine camp," Bradshaw said as the men collected their supplies. "Mr. Plummer expects authority and closure from this confrontation, and that's what he'll receive. Any resistance from the unionizers or their families merits disciplinary measures."

The men listened somberly. Prince, still standing in line for his gun, took out a tin of brilliantine and began combing it through his hair. Harvey's face was still and expressionless, though Jude could tell he was listening closely. Bradshaw rotated one of the rifles in his hands, inspecting for damage before reaching into his coat pocket and pulling out a box of bullets.

"I anticipate minimal hostility from this confrontation," Bradshaw said, feeding bullets into his rifle. "We have orders to deal with the unionizers, which encompasses the entire camp."

Jude saw Harvey shift out of the corner of his eye, but he said nothing.

"Any questions?" Bradshaw asked, more of a challenge than an inquiry. "Inspect your firearms and secure your holsters."

Bradshaw turned and began marching up the hill. Jude started to fall back, but Bradshaw's beefy arm whipped out and pushed Jude forward. He gave Jude a stern look, and Jude knew he would not get his preference of bringing up the rear. Harvey followed obediently nearby.

"What have you shot at before?" Jude asked Harvey quietly as they climbed the hill. Though he still strode at the front of the group, Jude had fallen back a few paces from Bradshaw, who charged up the hill on his powerful legs.

"What?" Harvey asked.

"You said you've never shot at a man," Jude said. "So what have you shot?"

"Plenty."

"Be straight with me, kid," Jude said. "You've never touched a gun in your life, have you?"

"I don't tell lies," Harvey answered stiffly.

"Ok, well—what have you shot? Anything that moved?"

Harvey glanced at the other men, but they were all several paces behind. Jude nudged his elbow.

"I've used a gun," Harvey said finally. "I shot a few on our farm."

"Alright, that's something. Depending on what you shot at."

"Pigs."

"Pigs?"

"I was the one who put them down."

Jude ran a hand over his nose and mouth, laughing. Bradshaw looked sharply behind him, and Jude whispered to Harvey, "Point blank? Or did you paint little bullseyes on their heads and try your aim?"

Harvey's hands tightened into fists, his face flushed. "Tell Bradshaw, and I swear to God—"

Jude threw his hands up. "Don't look at me, kid. It's no skin off my nose if you can't shoot the broad side of a barn. Just make sure you—"

"Approaching the mine!" Bradshaw announced in a hoarse whisper. He wheeled around, facing the men. "Holsters loose. Eyes alert."

"Alright, Harvey, you're going to have to touch your gun now," Jude murmured, reaching down and loosening the snap on his own holster. All mirth had left his voice and face, and a numbness saturated him from head to toe. The rigidity slithered from his back and shoulders, and he accepted impassiveness as a substitute for calm.

The men were quiet now, their arms hanging with simulated repose by their sides. They only disclosed agitation in the way their hands occasionally closed over the gun handles poking from the holsters, as if ensuring that they were still there. Prince was the only exception; he had his hands locked behind his head, flanking his neck with the diamond shape of his bent arms.

"How many raids has Bradshaw led?" Harvey asked quietly as they continued forward.

"Hell if I know. He's been with the Baldwin-Felts for ages," Jude replied. His hand itched to dip into his back pocket for the flask.

"Washer!" Bradshaw called, trying to keep his voice low but sounding strident nonetheless.

"With me, kid," Jude said, motioning to Harvey. They both strode forward to stand by Bradshaw.

"We go up to the mine," Bradshaw said, pointing up ahead. "The shift's about to start. Stay alert. There's something going on here."

The camp was eerily quiet and nearly motionless. More than anything, it resembled Jude's own mine camp after the Baldwin-Felts had raided: silent, still, almost abandoned. Jude's mouth felt mossy and he ran his tongue around his gums to stimulate saliva. He had learned years ago that he could not afford to think, much less reminisce, during raids.

The men's boots crunched through the pebbly, loose earth that carpeted the ground. With no foliage to buffer the wind, the men were whipped with cold, powerful gusts that tightened their skin and their lungs. Bradshaw led the men through the center of the camp on their way toward the mine.

As the Baldwin-Felts agents passed through the camp, the sound of soft-spoken conversations behind the cabin doors shied away till only the clucking chickens and the men's pounding boots were audible. From his peripheral vision, Jude could see Harvey surveying the camp openly, his eyes landing on every cabin and every face that peered fleetingly from the doorways.

Jude strode forward to keep up with Bradshaw. Their remaining trek passed in complete silence. Even Prince walked solemnly, his eyes alert and dancing but his mouth, for once, closed into a straight line.

Men were milling about in front of the mine, some beginning to enter the cavern but most still collecting equipment for the shift. From a distance, Jude could see one man notice the approaching agents, and suddenly the miners began to move with urgency. Beside him, Bradshaw's pace faltered, then sped up. His hands tightened around the rifle he held. Jude's hand drifted toward his holster, feeling his heartrate accelerate.

Now some fifty yards away, they could clearly see the men beginning to take positions by the mine carts outside the cavern or crouching low by the smattering of scrubby bushes that grew stubbornly around the outskirts of the mine. Jude could hear the men behind him growing restless, murmuring to one another. He dared not take his eyes off the mine ahead, now thirty yards away. It was at this distance that he saw the barrel of a shotgun slip over the edge of the mine cart, and before he or the others could react, a deafening shot split the air. The agents all ducked simultaneously, Bradshaw swearing ferociously.

"Find cover!" Jude shouted.

Harvey had dropped to the ground, and Jude jerked him up by his forearm. "Run!"

Stumbling, Harvey rose to his feet as two more shots clapped like thunder. Jude and Harvey sprinted and threw themselves behind a low boulder at the edge of the road as they heard one of the men let out a cry of pain.

"Return fire!" Bradshaw barked. He had taken cover on the opposite side of the road, his back pushed against a diseased-looking hickory. His face was purple with rage as he twisted around the tree trunk, aimed, and fired. The miners ducked below their shelters, their own shouts now rivaling that of the agents.

"Someone's got to help him," Harvey said. His eyes were fixed on the road, where one of their men was clutching his side and wriggling pitifully in an attempt to reach shelter. Harvey began to rise, but Jude laid an iron-like grip on his shoulder.

"Let me go!" Harvey said, wrenching out of Jude's grasp.

Harvey lurched out onto the road, but in a flash another bullet found the man on the road, this time in the back of his skull. Jude leapt up and snatched the back of Harvey's shirt, yanking him to the ground as another shot rang out. They heard a crack as the bullet imbedded itself in the tree directly behind them. Jude could feel his nerves beginning to fray, and he turned on Harvey, who breathed fast and hard, frozen on the ground. Jude gripped the boy's shirtfront and shook him.

"No heroics," he shouted. "You do what I tell you!"

Harvey, ashen, nodded several times. Jude released him and pulled out his flask, tossing it to Harvey.

"Drink, before you puke everywhere."

As Harvey fumbled with the cap, Jude peered around the boulder again. Two of the other agents had come closer to Bradshaw and took aim at the miners while Bradshaw reloaded his rifle, pushing the bullets in with brutal force. Jude wouldn't look at the man lying dead in the middle of the road. He searched for Prince and eventually found him a few yards away shooting mechanically, his face completely washed of expression in the effort of concentration. Prince had a reputation as the best shot in the group; in a matter of minutes, he had shot down two or three miners who did not rise up again over the edge of their carts.

Harvey began to sputter and cough, and Jude turned in time to see him turning red in the face, flask in hand.

"Swallow!" Jude shouted.

Harvey's eyes closed and his Adam's apple bobbed for a few minutes, then he opened his eyes again.

"What the hell do you keep in there?" Harvey gasped.

Before Jude could answer, a shout from Bradshaw, piercing as a hawk's cry, sent gooseflesh crawling over Jude's arms. A split second later, the world erupted. Clods of earth flew everywhere. Jude's ears rang and white spheres clouded his vision. Dazed, Jude looked at the road and saw a crater where the fallen agent had been mere seconds before. Dust billowed everywhere, and some of the nearby trees caught spark and began to smolder. Bradshaw, knocked to the ground, stumbled to his feet and began shouting. Jude could not make out what he said. Harvey, who had rolled over on his side with his hands clamped over his ears, pulled himself up, looking as stupefied as Jude felt.

Dynamite. Dynamite. Dynamite. The word repeated itself like an overdue omen in Jude's head. In a rush, the sounds around him amplified and the boom of shouts and shots once again dizzied his head. Now, he could make out the syllables of Bradshaw's roars: Retreat.

Chapter Three

ude flicked the knife across the wood, chips flinging off in different directions. He could hear Bradshaw's roar in Plummer's lodge, occasionally broken by the defensive stammering of the manager. The knife swiped faster and harder, and Jude hissed as the blade grazed the side of his thumb. He dropped the nub of wood and the knife, sucking at the stripe of blood streaming from his hand.

"Calmer. Calmer," Jude muttered to himself. He tugged a crumpled handkerchief from his pocket and pressed it against the cut. Waiting for the blood to clot, Jude flicked open his flask to dribble a bit over the wound, but he found it empty. Glowering, he knotted the handkerchief around his hand and stood up. Harvey approached from the lodge.

"Bradshaw wants you," Harvey said.

"I've half a mind to wait till he cools down some," Jude said.

"That didn't happen at the mine, did it?" Harvey asked, gesturing to the bandaged hand.

"Don't worry about it," Jude said. He picked up the bit of wood from the ground and wiped the knife's blade on his pant leg before stowing both away in his pocket.

"What's he been saying?" Jude asked as he and Harvey strode toward the lodge.

"I thought you could have heard from where you were sitting. Bradshaw's breathing fire because he thinks Plummer let word get out we were coming. He swears he said nothing."

Jude grunted. "Yeah, sure. What gets me is the guns. Can't buy those at the camp store."

"Then where'd they get them?"

"That's the kicker, ain't it?"

They came upon the lodge door, and Jude let out a gust of air as he rested his hand upon the knob. He hated getting drawn into Bradshaw's tempers. Someone else would be better suited to calm the old bull and put a strategy into effect.

The lodge was large and rectangular, a single, open room forming the whole first floor. It was impressive yet spartan, with few furnishings to distract from the overwhelming element of wood. Jude was struck by the difference between this wooden cavern and the home Mr. Wagner had built for himself and his wife, just over the mountain. The Wagners' place had seemed like a dollhouse propped on the side of the hill, where this seemed more like a monument of industry.

At the other end of the room stood a giant fireplace armored in river rock, and it was by this that they found Bradshaw and

Plummer. Bradshaw, though sitting in an oversized armchair, looked more tense than if he were stalking the floor. Plummer stood rigidly with his back to the roaring fire. He was a wiry man, nearly half the size of Bradshaw, with a band of wispy blond hair wrapping the back of his head like a parched crown of laurels.

"Washer," Bradshaw said. "Good. I have information for you."

Jude stepped over to the fire, feeling suddenly the deep cold that had creeped into his bones while sitting outside. He nodded to Plummer, who smiled tightly and edged off to the side.

"I'm all ears," Jude said, rubbing his hands over the flames.

"Face me, then, if it's not too much to ask."

Jude turned, content to let the fire's warmth expand across the back of his legs and torso. Bradshaw's face could curdle fresh milk. His temples and jowls were framed in dark red, with veins worming across the brow. The deep lines around his mouth seemed more like ridges furrowing a rock than wrinkles in flesh. Harvey had wisely remained all the way on the other side of the room, out of earshot.

"I have sent a telegram ordering fresh supplies and mounts, to arrive tomorrow afternoon. We will retaliate as rapidly as possible to allow the miners minimal time to reassemble." He rose abruptly, coming near to Jude by the fireplace. "I will not skulk and sneak back to that place," he said in a low voice. "I have never ordered a retreat in my career and I did so only after watching dynamite plaster a man's corpse into the trees. We will return fully equipped, and I'll be damned if I leave a single unionizer standing."

Jude said nothing, rubbing his hands slowly up and down the

side of his thighs. He could feel Bradshaw's eyes boring into him like a rod of hot iron.

"You will facilitate the men's target practice tomorrow morning as we wait on reinforcement," Bradshaw said. "The shooting today was disgusting." He lifted his chin, now examining Jude down the bridge of his crooked brown nose. "Speaking of which, I didn't notice you taking any shots, Washer."

Harvey, who had been standing inconspicuously on the other side of the room, looked up. Jude could spot Plummer watching as well, now standing at the very edge of the fireplace.

"I was occupied with Morgan," Jude said, regretting his words as soon as Bradshaw's granite eyes swiveled to bore into the boy. "He wanted to help our man," Jude added lamely.

Bradshaw straightened so that he no longer loomed over Jude. "We've got no place for heroes at Baldwin-Felts. Only fighters."

By sunrise, Jude had set up rows of straw bales against the side of a hill, scrubbing crude bullseyes onto the fronts with a lump of charcoal. As he finished, he could hear Bradshaw rousing the men in Plummer's lodge; they had all slept in the large lower room, this time with one excess bedroll. Bradshaw had made a display of unrolling it in front of the men last night, holding up the limp piece of cloth and meeting each of their eyes.

"Is this who we are?" Bradshaw had asked them, his voice unusually restrained. Jude, sitting with his back against the hearth, carved once more at the piece of wood, this time making his etches slow and careful. His hand ached from the cut that morning.

Bradshaw shook the bedroll. The men, some standing near

the fire like Jude, some already sitting atop their own bedrolls, stared wordlessly. Harvey, standing a few feet from Jude, had his hands tucked under his armpits, the bones of his jaw outlined clearly against his skin.

When no men spoke up, Bradshaw crumpled the bedroll into a ball and flung it to the ground. "This is not who we are," Bradshaw shouted, making several of the men flinch. "We are not antagonized. These hillbilly goons haven't had a newspaper reach them in the past half-century, or else they'd know what kind of fight they've picked. Tomorrow, we introduce them to the Baldwin-Felts they'll remember for a century to come."

Prince's eyes shone. Many of the men nodded grimly, grunting their agreement. Jude whittled at the nub of wood, making small notches at the top for a pair of ears. Whether they were to be long and pointed, like a hare's, or the broad round ears of a bear, he had not yet decided. He would do just about anything to tune out Bradshaw's tirades. There were times when he thought about other things he could be doing instead, working jobs that didn't involve so much shooting and screaming militants. Jude thought of his rented room back in Bluefield—comfortless, but at least he would have some solitude.

This morning, as the men streamed out of the lodge, they were not bleary-eyed and cantankerous as the morning before. Today, they approached with a stiffened gait and heads held up rather than bowed over their chests while yawning.

"Washer will be leading your target practice," Bradshaw said, bringing up the rear. His fury had calmed since the night before, but there was something about Bradshaw's poise that was deadlier, like a pillar of iron pulled from the forge and cooled until hardened and black. When the men were deposited before Jude,

Bradshaw turned on his heel and walked back toward the lodge. Plummer waited with two saddled and bridled ponies, which they mounted before disappearing down the road.

Jude, who had been leaning against a tree in the tomcat pose he was known for, straightened and flicked his thumb at the bales of hay. "Alright, let's get this right the first time," Jude said once Bradshaw was out of sight. "You see the target. Shoot it."

Though Jude had a reputation for several things, he was far from the best shot in the group—that title belonged to Prince. The men took their revolvers and staggered themselves before the row of targets. Prince stood on the farthest end from Jude, yet Jude could smell the oily cologne of his brilliantine drifting from that distance. Jude rubbed his nose against his sleeve.

"Okay, fire," he said.

A cacophony of shots vibrated the air, and puffs of dust and stubble jumped from the straw bales.

"Go through your bullets," Jude said. "Then we'll take a look at the targets."

As the shots continued, Jude searched the line of men for Harvey. He spotted him close to Prince, face stony but with sweat already glistening on his temples. Jude ran his hand over his eyes—bloodshot from too little sleep—and ambled behind the men to the other end of the row.

"How'd you do?" Jude asked. The other shots died suddenly as all the men fired their last bullet.

"I think I hit it," Harvey said flatly, letting his arm hang loose by his side.

"Let's find out," Jude said. Louder, he said: "Guns down. Inspect your target."

Jude and Harvey strode down to the target, about twenty feet away. Jude knelt and inspected the straw for indentations where the bullets would bury. He found one, nicking the very corner of the bale, and he could see several pits in the earth behind the bale where he knew he would find the other bullets. He glanced up at Harvey, whose face had fallen.

"Would it help if it oinked?" Jude asked.

"Go to hell."

Jude straightened, eyebrows raised. Harvey turned to walk back, then reeled around again. "How can you crack jokes?" he demanded in a low voice. "Didn't you see his blood on the trees?"

Jude had no idea what Harvey meant at first, then remembered their man who had fallen in the road the day before. He tried to relive that scene—the raid, the shooting, the dynamite. He had seen the smoke, the dust, and the basin of earth where the agent's body had been mere seconds before. He remembered the red sparks painting the trees and catching the limbs on fire. But no—perhaps the redness had not been from the sparks.

Jude looked Harvey in the eye, who was watching him with his brows drawn close together. Just a kid—he understood nothing.

"Take ten steps back and shoot again," Jude said, raising his voice for the other men. "Come on," he said to Harvey.

"Don't you want me shooting?"

"Stop talking back to me," Jude snapped. "I'll give you to Bradshaw if you keep that up. And trust me, he'd drill you so hard you'll wish you were one of your pigs from back home."

Harvey's scowl eased a little, but he said nothing. Jude led the way back to the lodge and searched out the icebox. He stuck his head inside and fished out a jar of milk. He sniffed it before sloshing it into two ceramic cups sitting out on the table.

"What's this for?" Harvey asked.

"Well, since you didn't seem so keen on what I offered you yesterday, I figured this was more to your taste," Jude replied, sipping the milk. It tasted sweet to him, almost sugary in comparison to the moonshine he had been lapping the past few days. The milk was cold, so cold that it had fine crystals of ice swirling in it. Jude's teeth ached, and he smiled. Harvey took a deep drink too, and his face relaxed.

"How'd you get a hold of that motor oil, anyway?" Harvey asked, the corners of his mouth glazed with milk.

"Motor oil?" Jude repeated, laughing.

"S' bout what it tasted like," Harvey said, his voice distorted as he tipped the ceramic cup over his mouth. Jude could hear his loud gulps.

"It's not as hard to find as you think," Jude said, rotating the cup in his hands. He thought back to the first time he tried moonshine; one of his pals back in Bluefield, a paperboy in the Wagners' neighborhood, had brought over a bottle, and between the two of them they finished it off late one night, telling jokes and making fun of the rich families that lived in the neighborhood. Though he had been violently sick the next morning and had to hide his newfound habit from the Wagners, Jude had exalted in the numbing alcohol and found respite from his still-fresh grief. Seemed like every night, Willis's face made its way into Jude's dreams. It came up during the day, too. He'd see it floating in windows or flashing across the face of a passing child. Moonshine didn't stop him imagining the face from time to time—but it helped him not to care. That experimentation with alcohol was child's play compared to what he consumed after joining the Baldwin-Felts.

"Does Bradshaw know about it?" Harvey asked.

Jude chuckled, licking up the last drops of milk that glazed the inside of the cup. "Bradshaw knows a lot of things about me," Jude answered. "It's about what he chooses to ignore."

Harvey placed his cup down and rested his elbows on the table, looking at Jude with a frankness that made him uncomfortable. "What is it about you that makes him give exceptions?" Harvey asked.

Jude grabbed a chair and straddled it, resting his arms over the back of the chair. Outside, he could hear the shots still ringing out; now and then, he could pick out the sound of Prince shouting orders. Prince in charge—not a pleasant thought.

"Well?"

Jude dug at the dirt underneath his fingernails. "Bradshaw doesn't make exceptions, to me or anybody else," he answered. "You realize where these agents were before they became Baldwin-Felts? Some still have bedbugs from their prison cots."

"So, you're telling me you could get away with anything."

"Sometimes I wish we couldn't," Jude said, looking down at his hands. He glanced up. "But we can."

Dust rose from the gravel path leading up to the lodge. Soon, Bradshaw and Plummer appeared on horseback, this time with a couple of ponies following behind on a tether. Jude shaded his eyes with his hand and looked up at the sun: just after noon.

"Gather round," Bradshaw shouted.

The men, now idling by the straw targets, became alert and moved forward. Bradshaw dismounted from his horse and walked back to the two other ponies they had brought. Both were laden with large, heavy canvas bags. Bradshaw loosened one of the buckles and reached his arm into the bag.

"Our weapons of war," he said, and drew out a glinting black machine gun.

Mutters rippled through the men. Prince pushed to the front, running his hands through his greased hair and grinning rabidly. Jude, who had sidled up with Harvey beside him, became very still.

"Not my preferred form of delivery," Bradshaw continued, thrusting the machine gun into the arms of the closest man, "and I could only get my hands on five. But my guess is they'll leave an impression. Prince?" he asked, holding a gun out.

Prince ran his tongue over his teeth, shaking his head. "No, sir. No-o, sir."

Bradshaw frowned. "What's the matter? Can't shoot a machine?"

"I can shoot one, you better believe it," Prince said. A smile flicked on and off his mouth like a spasm, and he shifted his weight from foot to foot. "Hot damn, yes," Prince said. "I can shoot a machine."

"What's the problem, then?"

Jude shoved his hands deep into his pockets. "Leave him with a rifle," he said. Prince with a machine gun was a thought that turned him queasy.

Bradshaw turned, noticing Jude. His mouth formed a long, straight line, and he looked at Jude for several moments. He must have collected something from Jude's demeanor, for he withdrew the offered machine gun and shoved it into another man's hands.

"Very well," Bradshaw said. "You're best with the rifle, anyway."

Bradshaw paced in front of the men, watching as they handled their guns or stowed bullets in their pockets. "Our reputation as Baldwin-Felts hangs on the retaliation we take today," Bradshaw said. "We were hired to execute discipline to these unionizers, and they had the gall to release fire onto us before a civil word was spoken." Bradshaw's breath was heavy and audible, and the sinews of his neck stood out. "Or do you men need reminding of how Thomas Robinson was blasted into pieces by dynamite?" He scowled and spat into the dirt.

Jude's eyes fixed on the glob of saliva bubbling in the dirt, thinking only that he had not been able to remember the man's name till Bradshaw had said it. He allowed memories of the attack yesterday to resurface, trying to linger on the man's—Robinson's—pitiful crawl to safety, followed by the deafening explosion that had daubed the trees with human entrails. Jude tried to summon pity, even anger, but instead felt only a leaden weight at the bottom of his stomach.

By contrast, the other men had caught some scent of aggression off of Bradshaw and were growing excited. They gripped their firearms with white knuckles, faces set and bodies tense. Jude turned to look at Harvey, who was also gripping his gun; his head was turned in the direction of the mine camp.

Chapter Four

Weak, slushy snow began to fall as the Baldwin-Felts approached the camp, the flakes settling onto Jude's lashes before evaporating a moment later. It was probably the last snow of the season. The other men squinted up at the sky with a scowl, but Jude liked the hush that the snow brought. The forest went quiet and the curtain of white flakes turned everything gauzy, like a dinner table draped with cheesecloth.

Jude and Prince were placed on a hill overlooking the mine camp; Prince gripped his rifle, tasked with the duty of picking off surprise attackers. Bradshaw had ordered Jude to join Prince under the pretense of playing second sniper, though Jude knew that Bradshaw only wanted Prince supervised. On many occasions, Bradshaw had praised Prince's shooting skills—never in Prince's presence—but he also had a disdain for Prince's lack of control: one of the few points Jude and Bradshaw agreed on.

Bradshaw and the other men approached the camp from the main road. The miner's camp was eerily still, and Jude did not see anyone moving outside. One of Plummer's men had reported the night before that several of the miners had abandoned the camp; those that remained, he said, were holed up in their cabins. Jude watched as the Baldwin-Felts entered the camp, Bradshaw on his tall horse, the others on foot. He could just make out Harvey in the middle, holding a revolver but with his arms hanging loose by his sides.

"Here we go," Prince said, pulling his rifle forward and angling the barrel down at the camp.

Jude, who had pulled out his knife for whittling wood a while back, continued to carve, concentrating on steadying the slight tremor in his hands as he guided small strokes with the knife. Prince glanced over at him and snorted.

"Look who's so relaxed," he said, turning to look back down at the camp.

Jude smiled grimly to himself before closing his pocketknife and tucking the wood back into his pocket. Bradshaw was riding through the center of the camp, his head moving rigidly back and forth. No one emerged from the cabins. Without warning, Bradshaw pulled his rifle out and, pointing the barrel straight into the sky, let off two booming shots. He shouted to the men, and they dispersed around the camp, beating on locked doors or, on the more brittle cabins, breaking in directly. Screams began to erupt, and Jude saw the agents drag men and their families out of the cabins.

Prince took a shot, and Jude jumped at the deafening noise and saw a man drop far below at the door of his own cabin. He heard wailing and saw arms reach out from the doorway before recoiling shakily. Jude closed his eyes, letting the snowflakes melt on his eyelids and slicken his lashes.

When Jude opened his eyes, he found himself searching for Harvey in the scene below. The miners were beginning to swarm out into the open, like ants surging from a kicked anthill. Some were forcefully dragged out while some fled on their own. A few of the miners had guns and made poor shots at the agents; others charged thoughtlessly into fistfights before being gunned down with the machine guns. Soon, the miners and Baldwin-Felts were clustered close enough together that Prince stopped making shots. He watched for a few minutes, running his tongue several times over his lips, then he shoved his rifle aside.

"I don't know about you, Washer, but I'm getting down there," he said, standing and pulling his revolver out of his holster. He shot a grin at Jude, then ran down the hill with a whoop.

Jude bent over his knees, pressing the palms of his hands into his forehead. He could hear the chaos down below, an ugly contrast to the snowy tranquility where he sat. Jude breathed heavily through his nostrils, feeling the light, momentary sting of snowflakes landing on his skin before melting. He tried to disconnect and found he could not. The drill of the machine guns and the shrieks of fear filled his head.

The fact that he was alone now sprung into realization, and the temptation to run down the other side of the mountain, away from the Baldwin-Felts and the miners, expanded in Jude's mind till, for a few moments, he felt convinced he would do it. For years Jude had imagined leaving the Baldwin-Felts and stepping away from the violence—finding a way to make himself into the sort of man he had thought, mistakenly, that the Baldwin-Felts would turn him into.

An eruption of noise below sprung Jude out of his reverie. In a split second, a handful of miners were mown down by one of the machine guns, and sparks flared where the bullets struck the tin roofs of the shacks. Many dead bodies littered the ground, some of them women. A man knelt beside the body of a woman, rolled her over, then staggered backwards. It was Harvey.

Jude rose and left the hilltop, discarding the idea of abandoning the Baldwin-Felts like a child leaves a shop window displaying too-expensive toys. He drew out his revolver, running down the hill and heading straight for Harvey. Jude's heart hammered once more, and he felt sick to his stomach as the noise grew louder and the blood became more visible on the miners' bodies.

"Harvey!" Jude shouted, ducking behind a shed as a stray bullet whizzed past.

"Jude?" Harvey's voice called back, sounding hoarse.

Jude darted out and rushed to where Harvey remained kneeling on the ground, skidding to a stop beside the boy and grasping his arm with an iron grip. Jude yanked Harvey aside and pushed him up against the side of a cabin, away from the clearing where bullets shot back and forth.

"You can't stay in one place," Jude panted, releasing Harvey's arm with a scowl. "You want to get shot, idiot?"

Harvey scrubbed his hands over his face, looking pale. He glanced back at the woman on the ground: her mouth drooped open and her eyes stared glassily into the sky. Jude felt bile rise in his throat, and he grabbed Harvey's arm once more.

"Get moving," he said. "We can't stay here."

The pair, bent over as they ran, moved toward the outskirts of the camp. Somewhere, Jude could make out Prince's shrill laughter over the din of the gunfire. When Jude glanced over his shoulder, he saw one of the cabins suddenly bloom with color as it caught fire. Jude swore and Harvey turned, his legs halting as he caught sight of the flaring cabin. A second later, and the cabin beside it caught flame. Jude caught a look in Harvey's eyes, the same look that had come over his face when he tried to sprint into the road to save the shot miner. Jude gripped his arm just as Harvey pulled forward and forced Harvey to face him.

"Let go!" Harvey yelled.

Jude shook Harvey's shoulders. "You'll get killed if you keep pulling these stunts!"

Harvey, despite his youth, was bigger than Jude and wrenched free, sprinting back to the cabins. Jude watched Harvey rush inside one cabin, but he reemerged empty-handed. The one beside still had its door shut, and Harvey thrust himself into the door. A second later, and several people rushed out, coughing, fleeing straight past Harvey and disappearing into the woods.

Jude made to move toward Harvey, but he was cut short as a girl ran past with Prince at her heels. She let out a scream as Prince grabbed her and pushed her to the ground, laughing. He started to pull the girl by her hair away from the middle of the clearing.

"Prince!" Jude shouted. The adrenaline was pumping strong now, and he yanked Prince off the girl with an ease that surprised himself. "You're paid to work, that's it," Jude spat, pushing Prince roughly in the chest. "You understand?"

Prince's doglike grin flickered. "She's all yours," Prince said, sweeping an arm toward the girl, who was scrambling to her feet. Prince glanced at the girl, flashing his lupine teeth, then ran back into the middle of the camp.

The girl darted forward and let out another scream, stumbling as a bullet struck her arm. Hardly knowing what he was doing, Jude rushed forward and pulled the girl behind a cabin. She struggled wildly, sobbing.

"Let go! Let go!" she screamed.

"Be still, you'll make it worse," Jude said, pinning the girl's arms to her side, careful not to clutch the wound. He looked into her face and his heart stopped as recognition hit him. In her eyes and the shape of her jaw he saw a semblance of Mam Myers. The oldest Myers girl flickered into memory and a million thoughts darted through Jude's brain as he tried to remember her name.

"Florrie?"

The girl did not seem to hear him but wrestled against his grasp with surprising strength, crying hysterically.

"I'm not here to hurt you," Jude said. "Please—be still—Florrie?"

The girl looked up at him with wide, bloodshot eyes, and Jude felt gooseflesh rise on his arms.

"Where's your ma?" Jude asked, unable to tear his eyes from the girl's face.

"Who are you?" Florrie sobbed, and Jude felt his heart skip as the Irish lilt came out in her quavering voice. A smile, shaky but relieved, broke over his face, and he suppressed a sob rising in his throat. So, the Myerses had made it out all those years ago. The smile fell away, though, when Jude realized what it would mean to tell her who he was. He released Florrie's arms and she took a step back, but did not run away.

"How do you know me?" she asked, placing her palm over her bleeding arm.

Jude let himself look at her and felt his throat tighten. She was thin and dirty, but had grown into a beautiful girl. She looked to be sixteen or so—near the age Willis would have been. They had been close playmates. If things had been different...

"You may not remember me," Jude said. He swallowed, and it hurt his throat. Snow landed on Florrie's hair, and he could see the blood seeping through her fingers. "But you may remember—do you remember Willis?" His voice rasped as he said his name aloud, for the first time in years.

Florrie's lips parted, a gust of her breath forming a cloud between them. "Jude? Washer?"

Jude felt pleasure and shame at the same time at hearing his own name, spoken from someone who had known him from that far-away past. "Let me help you," Jude said.

From a distance, Bradshaw's voice roared. "Washer!"

Florrie stepped backward a few steps, her eyes locked on Jude the way a doe watches a hunter. Jude's heart sank as he saw the realization dawning in her eyes. Florrie turned and ran.

Jude ran after her in a frenzy, powered by an overwhelming urgency to follow. She might lead him to Mam Myers. What he would do then he did not have the clarity of mind to plan; but this time, at least, he would make sure that they did not fall victim to the Baldwin-Felts.

Without warning, the cabin nearest to Jude suddenly collapsed in flames, spitting sparks into Jude's path as he skidded to a halt. He threw up his arms to protect his eyes; the flare of heat alone made his skin tingle. When Jude lowered his arms, Florrie was nowhere to be seen. All that met his eyes was the blazing remains of the cabin with snowflakes drifting down, only to melt mid-air.

Jude bent over, his breath coming in sporadic bursts. He pressed the heels of his hands into his eyes, finding them wet with tears. Half of him wanted to push forward and find Florrie and the rest of her family, but half of him still cringed at the look in Florrie's eyes. He didn't know if he could take that look from Mam Myers.

The gunfire, seeming distant now, was becoming intermittent. The miners were surely running out of ammunition. Jude wiped his eyes and stood up. Forces more powerful and kind than himself had spared the Myerses from the raid over ten years ago: Jude would leave them in the care of those same fates. Jude turned away from the burning cabin, now just a smoldering heap, and reminded himself of Harvey. He had to be found, and kept from killing himself.

As he emerged back into the open, a miner darted into a doorway and took a shot at him. Jude just barely dodged it, but did not shoot back. The shot served to refuel his adrenaline and reminded Jude of the danger he was still in. He moved more carefully back to the spot where he had last seen Harvey. Many of the cabins, like the one he had left, were already burned to the ground.

Jude could see Bradshaw and a handful of agents clustered near the back of the camp, closer to the mines, taking shots at a cluster of miners who had formed a stronghold. Jude saw several Baldwin-Felts lying dead on the ground.

Harvey appeared out of nowhere, ushering two bent-over old women out of a cabin. Their faces were creased with fear, staring at Harvey with looks of bewilderment, but nonetheless hurrying out of the camp and heading for the woods. Jude started to call Harvey's name, but a second later and the boy had dashed over to the next building, smaller and shabbier than the others, with its roof ablaze. Harvey beat down the door and a goat charged out, its hide singed, and several chickens fluttered through the opening. Harvey ducked inside.

"Harvey!" Jude yelled, running forward. "Idiot, get out of there!"

When Harvey emerged, he held a half-burnt hen in one arm and was tugging at a rope, at the end of which was a suckling pig.

"Take it," Harvey said, shoving the chicken into Jude's arms. Harvey took both hands and pulled at the rope.

"You've lost it," Jude said, looking with some disgust at the wilted hen in his arms; the creature was half-dead already, and Jude placed it on the ground. "They're animals!"

The pig abruptly darted forward, squealing, and disappeared into the trees. Panting some, eyes red from smoke, Harvey watched it go.

"Come on," Harvey said. "You've got to help me."

"Doing what?" Jude demanded. "Saving more livestock?"

Harvey wiped his mouth with his sleeve. There was no more nervous panic in his face, but instead something like anger.

"I'm not standing for this," Harvey said. "I'm getting these people out of here. To hell with Bradshaw—to hell with the Baldwin-Felts! This is all insanity!"

"Well that's not going to cut it, kid."

Harvey and Jude turned to see Prince striding toward them, twirling his revolver around his finger and showing all his feral teeth.

"He's in shock, Prince," Jude said, stepping in front of Harvey. "Doesn't know what he's saying."

Prince shoved Jude aside. "Like hell," he growled, and with one blow dropped Harvey to the ground.

Chapter Five

A second later and Prince had Harvey pinned to the dirt, gripping his neck, pressing his two thumbs deep into the hollow of the boy's throat. Jude could hear Prince's heavy breathing and Harvey's frantic choking, his arms alternating between tugging at Prince's hands and aiming useless punches.

"You're both…damn…loons!" Jude yelled, shoving his shoulder against Prince so that he toppled off Harvey with a hot gasp of rage.

"Stay out of it!" Moisture sprayed from Prince's mouth. His hair dangled over his forehead in wet black spirals, the brilliantine reeking. He pushed the locks of hair off his brow with cracked fingernails, moving his glare between Harvey and Jude.

Jude tensed his hand, shaped to grab his revolver should he need it. Harvey propped on his elbows, gasping, his fingers roaming over the pink ring appearing around his neck. He and Jude were otherwise still, watching Prince as if he were a mad dog about to lurch forward, mouth foaming.

And then he did lurch forward, at Jude. He hurled a reckless punch that glanced off Jude's chin and ended up striking his shoulder. Jude's hand balled into a fist and he pulled back, landing a strike into Prince's gut. He could feel each bone in his hand compress and the joints crunch, but he felt nothing crack as his fist collided with Prince's diaphragm. A gust of foul-smelling breath came out of Prince and he staggered back, for a second his mouth gaping like a fish's as he struggled to refill his lungs with air. The next second, and they were locked together, Prince's arm wrapped around Jude's head, the crook of his arm pushing tight under Jude's chin.

"Back to your old tricks, Washer?" Prince panted into Jude's ear. "Turning on the Baldwin-Felts this time, is that it? Your daddy wasn't enough?"

The condensation of Prince's breath collected on Jude's skin. Jude was overcome with crawling revulsion as a surge of adrenaline coursed through his body. He threw off Prince's grip with sudden ease, and swiped a blind punch. It hit Prince on the left ear, a blow that sent him reeling.

Jude shook out his hand, wondering when he had last felt this good. He had so long depended on the moonshine to dampen his mind that he had forgotten the wild heat of adrenaline. Every muscle felt alive and limber, ready to move with liquid ease or harden into steel. Jude could feel the cloth fibers of his shirt skimming against his skin and could taste the cold in every pore.

His ears, prickling with a dozen sensations, heard the sound of Prince's gun sliding from its leather holster before he saw him lift the weapon, finger on the trigger. Jude recognized the threat indistinctly, as if he were facing a painting with Prince trapped in colored oils, the revolver nothing but a few gray strokes from a paintbrush. When the shot fired, he flinched, yet felt no pain. With surprise he realized that Prince, not he, bled, clutching his arm with a howl. Jude turned to see Harvey kneeling on the ground, his revolver poised in his hands and smoking.

The weight of a third pair of eyes settled on Jude's consciousness, and he turned to see Bradshaw watching from atop his horse across the camp, fury mounting in every line of his body as he caught sight of the smoking revolver in Harvey's hand and Prince bent on the ground, heaving with pain as blood drenched his sleeve.

"Morgan!" Bradshaw shouted, and his voice was like the roar of a charging bull.

Bradshaw's yell lifted Prince's head, and a smile wormed across his lips. He began to laugh.

The revolver in Harvey's hand dropped as his arm went limp. He panted heavily, the ring around his throat turning an ugly puce. Bradshaw had reared his horse around and was thundering in their direction. Harvey's head drooped so that his chin rested on his sternum. No sooner had his head lowered, however, and Prince reached over with his good arm and snatched the revolver off the ground.

"Harvey!" Jude shouted, but too late; Prince pressed the trigger, and a bullet zipped out and struck Harvey's shoulder, knocking him onto his back. For a second, Bradshaw reined in his horse, watching the scene with his crystal eyes darting back and forth. Then, he pulled his rifle out and settled it on his shoulder. The other agents and the miners, engaged in their own war, seemed miles away.

"Make one more move, and I'll kill you each on the spot," Bradshaw shouted.

Prince sat back on his heels and dropped the revolver, laughing again. Harvey, flat on the ground, did not move.

"Is he dead?" Bradshaw asked, eyes bent on Harvey.

Jude moved to the boy, stepping warily and watching Bradshaw closely. His heart thundered in his chest as he bent over Harvey. His shoulder was already soaked with blood, and his face had grown ashen. Harvey's eyes were squeezed shut, his mouth a tight straight line, and his breath shuddered through his nostrils in irregular bursts.

"Harvey," Jude said quietly, gripping the boy's hand. Harvey's eyes flicked open for a brief second, and his hand returned Jude's grasp with painful tightness. Jude could feel Harvey's muscles twitching all up and down his arm. His throat tightened. A different face floated into Jude's mind.

"He's alive," Prince shouted back to Bradshaw, his voice laced with disgust.

"Let him bleed out," Bradshaw said. He lowered the rifle and dismounted, leading the horse by the reins as he came nearer to Prince. "Bandage that arm, Prince," he commanded. "Washer— get away from him. We have no room for traitors here."

Bradshaw's words sank into Jude as water sinks into sand. He did not look up at Bradshaw, instead keeping his eyes locked on Harvey's face, twitching with pain and growing whiter by the minute.

Jude remembered his first meeting with Bradshaw as a boy of

seventeen. "I hear you turned over your entire camp," Bradshaw had said, Mr. Wagner standing in the background. "Shows a lot of gumption." Jude had been welcomed in as a traitor, but perhaps Bradshaw was right—there was no room for traitors anymore.

"Kid, we're going to get out of here," Jude said, so softly that he could barely hear himself speak. "I'm going to need you to work with me, Harvey. You hear me?"

Harvey's eyelids lifted painfully, and his gaze locked with Jude's.

"Washer," Bradshaw barked, kneeling beside Prince. "I said leave him."

Jude reached over Harvey and grasped the boy's revolver, his heart pounding. Harvey still watched him, his eyes looking like two immense dark pools in the expanse of his ashen face. Jude turned to look at Bradshaw and Prince, gun in hand. They watched him in return.

"Fine, put him out of his misery," Prince scoffed, holding his bleeding arm close to his body. "I told you, he'd gotten attached," he said to Bradshaw.

The look in Bradshaw's face was more comprehending. Jude could see Bradshaw reading the grip of the gun in his hand and the hardening expression that would surely be showing on his face. Realization spanned in Bradshaw's eyes.

"Washer!" he bellowed.

Jude lifted the gun in one fluid movement, barely taking pause to aim for fear that he would lose the momentum of courage. He fired and heard Bradshaw's shout of pain. Without looking to see where the shot landed, Jude slid his arm roughly under Harvey's torso and hoisted the boy up into a sitting position.

Harvey gasped and went even whiter, the consciousness fading from his eyes. Barely comprehending his own actions, Jude thrust the heel of his hand hard against Harvey's wounded shoulder. The boy's eyelids sprung back open, pain flaring in his eyes as he let out a cry of pain, but a flush returned to his skin.

Prince scrambled to his feet, streaming curses. Jude aimed another blind shot over his shoulder, and he heard Prince scuffle for cover. Jude risked a glance at them; Bradshaw was gripping his thigh, baring his teeth and barking at Prince to shoot. Bradshaw's horse stood, jittery, nearby. Harvey, though shaking, looked at Jude with revived alertness. Jude could see the adrenaline taking over and gambled on Harvey's strength.

"Up," Jude commanded, and hauled Harvey to his feet. Harvey's face tightened with pain but his legs held him. Jude curled his tongue behind his teeth and let out a shrill whistle; Bradshaw's horse tilted its ears toward Jude and danced nervously forward. With one arm strapped around Harvey's ribs, Jude grabbed the horse's reins. He craned his head back to look at Prince and Bradshaw. Bradshaw was dragging himself in the dust toward where his rifle laid on the ground, but Jude's heart stopped when he saw Prince down on one knee, revolver aimed at Jude's head. He pulled the trigger, but no bullet shot out.

Prince let out a savage scream and threw the gun aside. He rose to his feet and ran for them, his bloodied arm no longer held close to his body but pumping like the other.

"Get on!" Jude shouted.

He shoved Harvey forward and, muscles flooded with adrenaline, hoisted him up onto the horse. Jude grasped the reins tightly as the horse shied sideways, then leapt up onto the horse's back as Harvey pulled himself up, face creased with pain. Before he knew it, Prince was upon them, and Jude felt his talon-like grip on his thigh. Jude launched a kick into Prince's gut which sent him reeling backward.

"Shoot them! Shoot them!" Bradshaw was screaming, his voice taken to a shrill octave that Jude had never heard before. Harvey managed to straddle the horse, though now he slumped back against Jude's chest. Jude kicked his heels into the horse and they lurched forward. Harvey's head lolled on its neck, and Jude realized he had passed out; he hooked one arm around the boy's torso and held him in place as the horse surged into a gallop. Bradshaw continued to scream behind them.

Then, a shot: this time from Bradshaw's rifle, and Jude yelled as a bullet grazed the side of his bicep. He twisted in the saddle and shot one last futile bullet back before the horse plunged down the road, the camp melting out of sight.

The horse labored to move quickly with two men on its back, not to mention that the steep descent forced caution. Jude muttered urges under his breath to the horse, though he knew that demanding speed could result in peril. Harvey had still not regained consciousness, though Jude felt grateful not to listen to his pained breathing. He still bled openly, however, and while the horse maneuvered down the mountain, Jude pulled back the collar of Harvey's shirt to inspect the wound.

Jude had never considered himself a squeamish man, but the tatters of loose flesh around the bullet's entry made his stomach flip. There was no exit wound, which sent a flicker of anxiety through Jude. He had heard somewhere that healing was easier if a bullet went clean through; regardless of whether that was true or not, Jude dreaded having to retrieve the bullet lodged in Harvey's shoulder. He tugged a handkerchief out of his pocket and did his best to plug the wound. Not the most sanitary, maybe, but if the bleeding didn't stop fast, Harvey would be nothing but baggage for the horse to carry.

The road leveled out at last, and Jude kicked his heels into the horse again. He trotted at a pace that jolted Jude through his spine and would undoubtedly make things twice as uncomfortable for Harvey, were he conscious. As it was, Jude pushed aside his own discomfort and felt glad that they were no longer picking their way down the mountain with maddening slowness. Someone would follow. Which of the men Bradshaw sent after them, Jude could not guess, but he knew for certain that they would be chased before long.

Jude flicked the reins anxiously. The horse's coarse brown hide was beginning to lather, but he pushed forward into a canter. Jude tightened his grip on Harvey as he felt him beginning to shift on the horse. His other arm ached, but at least the bleeding seemed to have stopped.

Jude tried to remember what they had passed on the road up to the mine the day before, hoping for some shelter where he and Harvey could lay low for a day or two. His instinct was to keep moving and put as much distance between them and the other agents, but it was clear that Harvey would not be able to withstand travel for much longer. Jude recalled a path branching off from the main road about a mile down the mountain, and in his mind he weighed the options of investigation. At the worst, it could lead to a dead end where they might be cornered should the agents come up on them quickly. At the best, it might be an abandoned homestead where they could find shelter and perhaps a few supplies to treat Harvey's wound. Jude glanced over his shoulder, but there was neither sight nor sound of a chase. If anything, he felt more nervous.

They came upon the pebbly driveway quicker than Jude anticipated. Harvey let out a few groans, though he did not appear fully conscious. The blood from his wound was beginning to seep into Jude's own shirt, and his stomach clenched. Jude tugged the reins to the side and the horse veered off onto the pathway.

Twilight settled between the trees, sinking slowly like molasses dripping down the side of a jar. The trees bordered the path closely and cast tall shadows over Jude as they passed through. Jude let the horse tread slowly, wary of what they might find at the end of the road. Soon, however, the shape of a cabin and a small barn emerged through the purple shadows. It seemed almost abandoned till he picked out the flicker of a candle from one of the back windows in the cabin, and a few scrawny chickens roaming sleepily through the yard. Jude stopped the horse and watched tensely for several minutes, deliberating whether to turn back. He had spent his entire life in the Blue Ridge Mountains, and he knew enough about mountain folk to know that they were averse to unannounced strangers, and they might as soon open fire on Jude and Harvey as the men back at the mine.

Harvey slumped heavily against Jude, and he felt both the hot blood and a clammy sweat leaking from the boy. Heart in his throat, Jude tilted Harvey forward to lean on the horse's neck and dismounted quietly. Reins in hand, he led the horse slowly, slowly, up behind the barn, which had doors at both ends. Jude's eyes darted between the cabin, which he watched closely, and Harvey, who he steadied with his free hand.

Before even entering through the doors, Jude could tell the barn had not been used for some time and that no other animals were inside. He expected the hinges to creak loudly, but instead the door eased open with only a tired-sounding groan. Very little light entered the barn, though a few red ribbons from the sunset seeped in through the splintered walls. There were two low stalls on one side, presumably once for pigs or maybe a goat, and a narrow horse's stall and a storage area on the other side.

The horse shivered and let out a low whicker, seeming to sense rest at last. Jude patted the horse's neck, waiting for his eyes to adjust so that he might make out more clearly what resources were in the barn. The floor was dusty and dry, though he could see straw still heaped in the corners of the animal stalls. Jude went into the pig pen and found it swept clean. He brushed his boot against the corners of the stall to clear out any spider webs, then moved over to the shelves. They were mostly bare, except for a few coils of rope and a tin filled with an odorless ointment. A half-empty sack of grain slumped against the wall, and Jude took it over to the horse stall. He poured some of the grain into the trough, and the horse nickered softly, moving eagerly forward. Jude rubbed the horse's forehead, remembering his brief spell as a stable boy in Bluefield, grooming Dorothy Wagner's expensive palomino mare.

Jude tossed the grain sack into the pig pen, then came to the horse's side. With a grunt, Jude pulled Harvey off the horse's back, struggling to keep his balance as the boy's weight came fully upon him. Harvey's eyelids flickered, and he let out a moan.

"Easy," Jude said. "Help me out, kid, come on."

Jude half carried, half dragged Harvey over into the pig pen before easing him to the ground, resting his head on the sack of grain. Seeing that Harvey was settled, Jude got up again and moved the horse into the stall. The horse sniffed the grain before eating, breathing noisily. Jude eyed the saddle still strapped to the horse's back but decided he could not sacrifice removing the saddle in case they needed a quick escape.

Closing the stall door behind him, Jude moved to the front of the barn, peeking through the cracks in the boards. Though dark had scarcely fallen, whoever was inside the cabin had already blown out their candle and no more movement could be seen in the house. Judging by the condition of the yard and buildings, Jude guessed someone old lived here. He exhaled deeply, not realizing he had been holding his breath in the first place.

"Jude," Harvey whispered from the other side of the barn.

Jude went to the stall. He could barely make out Harvey's white face in the shadows.

"Where are we?"

"We're hiding," Jude answered, kneeling beside Harvey.

Harvey's head shifted on the grain sack. "Are they after us now?" he asked.

"Keep your voice down," Jude said. "For now, we're fine."

Harvey closed his eyes again. "Do you have any water?" he asked.

"Yeah," Jude answered, though he knew they had none. It occurred to him then to search Bradshaw's saddlebags, and he returned to the horse. The horse ignored him as he rummaged through the bags, finding extra bullets, a packet of jerky and hard biscuits, a wallet filled with papers that Jude couldn't read in the poor light. At last, he found a metal canteen.

"Hello, beauty," Jude said, wishing only that he might have found a small flask along with the water.

"Jude," Harvey said, his voice floating faintly from the other side of the barn. "Did you really turn your father over to the Baldwin-Felts?"

Chapter Six

Jude did not turn around at first, but held the cold metal canteen in his hands.

"I've turned a lot of people over to the Baldwin-Felts," Jude said. "Sit up some and take this water."

Harvey struggled to sit up, his face contorting. He took several gulps of water before closing his eyes and resting his head against the side of the barn, breathing heavily. "Doesn't really answer the question," he said.

Jude rubbed the bridge of his nose between his fingers. "You really think now is the time to get into each other's personal histories?"

"I could either listen to you or think about this bullet in my shoulder," Harvey said, his eyebrows drawn together in a wince of pain.

Jude sighed and eased himself onto the floor beside Harvey. It hit him all at once how exhausted he was. "Ok, let's have story time. My old man was a piece of shit, so I decided the easiest way to get rid of him was to turn him over to the Baldwin-Felts for unionizing the miners." Jude rubbed his hands together to stir warmth. "Happily ever after, the end."

"What about your ma? Did you have any brothers and sisters?"

"Ma died when I was a kid," Jude answered gruffly. "I...had a brother."

"Did you turn him over too?"

Jude was the barest second away from grabbing Harvey by the shirtfront with a stream of filthy words before his anger was doused with the iron smell of Harvey's blood. Jude tightened his hands into fists and breathed out slowly through his nostrils, trying to regain control.

"Willis wasn't around for the Baldwin-Felts," Jude said. "He was killed—before."

"In the mines?"

Yes, in a gas-filled pit, deep in the belly of the mines. Running from—

"My father killed him," Jude said.

Harvey did not speak up again, but took another swig of water before handing the canteen to Jude. Jude took a long drink, savoring the icy coolness as it trickled over his gums. He wiped his lips with his sleeve and capped the canteen.

"You need to sleep," Jude said to Harvey, his voice coming out unnaturally quiet, almost hoarse. "Unless you're willing to let me get that bullet out of your shoulder."

Even in the dim light of the barn, Jude thought he could perceive the color wash more from Harvey's face. "No—not tonight," he said, swallowing audibly.

"Suit yourself," Jude said. "It ain't going to get any better, though."

Jude wondered how exactly he'd go about extracting the bullet from Harvey's shoulder. During his time with the Baldwin-Felts, Jude had only practiced rudimentary first aid, no more than hastily wrapping a flesh wound in gauze. In the meantime, at least, he figured he could clean Harvey's shoulder.

"Help me get your arm out of that sleeve," Jude said, setting down the canteen. "Let's at least get a look at her."

Harvey obeyed wordlessly, but the process of extracting his arm from his sleeve was painful. Typically Jude would have just tore or cut the arm out of the sleeve, but it was already frigid in the barn and Harvey would need the shirt's warmth. Eventually they managed to pull the arm out of the sleeve, exposing the shoulder. Jude wished for a lantern, but even if there had been one, he would have felt uneasy lighting it in case the lodger in the cabin might see.

Dried blood caked Harvey's torso down one side. Jude brushed this off with his hand and it flaked off easily. Harvey kept his eyes closed and seemed to be concentrating on his breathing. As Jude's hand came closer to the shoulder, he brushed more lightly, unsure of exactly where the wound was. He found the handkerchief he had plugged into the wound earlier during their escape. The blood up by the shoulder was gummy, only half-dried, though there seemed to be no fresh blood.

He lifted the canteen and poured a small amount of water into his cupped palm, then dribbled this gingerly over the shoulder before wiping away the crust of blood. Harvey began to shiver, and Jude wondered if he was doing the right thing, or if the cold would take Harvey into shock—a term he had heard once but only vaguely understood. He shook this from his mind and continued to wash Harvey's shoulder. He had to trust his instincts, and his instincts said to get the wound cleaned up.

Jude soon had most of the blood rinsed away, and he cautiously pulled at the handkerchief plugging the wound. Harvey's eyelids flew open and he gasped. Jude's heartbeat thundered in his chest. On impulse, he tugged the handkerchief out of the wound, which began to bleed afresh.

"Oh, Jesus," Jude muttered. He searched his pockets for another handkerchief but he had none. "Harvey—Harvey— you got a hankie?"

"Coat pocket," Harvey answered through clenched teeth. "What the hell did you do that for?"

Jude shoved his hand into Harvey's coat pocket and drew out a wrinkled bandana. For all he could see, it might be filthy and smeared with grease, but he had nothing else to use. He rolled the bandana into a strip and wrapped it snugly around Harvey's shoulder.

"Help me get this shirt back on," Harvey grunted. "I'm freezing."

"Sure, sure," Jude said. He tried to keep his hands from shaking as he pulled down Harvey's shirt.

Shivering, Harvey settled back against the sack of grain. "What made you get me out of there in the first place?" he stammered.

"If you're thinking you're something special, you can go on and get that out of your brain," Jude said. He tossed the old blood-soaked handkerchief into the corner and kicked some loose straw over it.

Harvey closed his eyes and pulled his good arm over his chest, sinking deeper into his coat. "That ain't what I think," he mumbled. "But a man doesn't toss his livelihood aside for nothing."

Jude settled back against the wall and fingered his own arm. It smarted where the bullet had grazed it, and Jude tugged his arm out of his sleeve to inspect it. Same as when he inspected Harvey, he could discern very little about the wound, but he rinsed it with a bit of water to clear away the dried blood. It was a shallow wound and didn't worry him much. He pretended to keep inspecting it, though, to avoid answering Harvey.

"The Baldwin-Felts aren't what I thought they'd be," Harvey said. His eyes were still closed, and his voice had grown quieter. "The recruiters called themselves deputies."

Jude smiled to himself. "Sounded pretty good to a farm boy, did it?" he asked.

He expected Harvey to rile, but instead he only murmured, "Yeah. It did."

Jude pulled his arm back into his shirt and tucked his hands into his armpits. "You ain't the first to fall for it. You go in thinking you're about to do some good, then you work at it for years before you realize maybe you signed up for something that ain't what you wanted."

Jude concentrated on a crack in the barn wall where a sliver of moonlight leaked through. At the time when he first met Bradshaw, Jude had spent the past three years in Wagner's rich neighborhood, working different jobs. At first, Jude had been amazed by the wealth and comfort that surrounded his new life with the Wagners; even as an errand boy, he had been given a comfortable room in the staff wing in the Wagner's home and had open access to Mr. Wagner's private library, though Jude was never much of a reader. He had meat to eat every day, and in the summers, Mrs. Wagner would let Jude have leftover ice cream from her parties.

But it only took a few weeks for Jude to realize he did not fit well into the city life. He disliked school and church, finding different ways to sneak out of both. Mr. Wagner took Jude in as a charity project—likely from the influence of his wife—and tried to open educational and social doors for him, saying he recognized "a humanitarian streak" in Jude.

When Bradshaw showed up, Jude had not found it difficult to leave the Wagners and join the band of Baldwin-Felts. To his young eyes, the Baldwins represented action and power, and he had jumped on the chance. Though Jude liked to think he was the shrewder being, he knew he had fallen for the exact same illusion as Harvey.

He glanced over at Harvey, but the boy was asleep. Jude shifted against the wall, trying to find a more comfortable position. His ears were so cold that he could no longer feel them, and the exposed skin about his neck and wrists were clammy. He could see Harvey shivering in his sleep. Jude took off his coat and laid it over the boy's legs, then exited the stall to pace up and down the barn. He kept his wounded arm by his side, but swung the other arm and stomped his feet, trying to stir the blood. He felt weariness heavy in his brain and limbs, but he was too nervous to try and sleep.

Jude walked up to the horse and rubbed its neck, realizing with a twinge of guilt that he had not given the horse any water. He retrieved the canteen and weighed it experimentally in his hand; he had used almost half for him and Harvey, but he sloshed the rest into the horse's trough. It was barely enough to cover the bottom of the trough, but the horse lapped at it eagerly. Jude glanced at the saddle still on its back; he knew the kind thing would be to remove the saddle and give the horse a rubdown, but Jude was anxious to have the horse ready to leave at a moment's notice. He felt twice as nervous that the Baldwin-Felts had not yet showed up in search of them.

Jude stroked the coarse horsehair, and the warmth of the animal and the rhythmic stroking soon settled his mind. The water was already gone, but the horse continued to nose around in the trough. Jude rested his forehead against the horse's neck, a wave of weariness breaking over him as he realized the impact of his actions. He would be a man on the run for an indeterminable amount of time, without an income and without even the ability to stay in one place for long. Jude knew well Bradshaw's brand of wrath, and he was sure he would be hunted just as if he were an escaped unionizer. He had seen the Baldwin-Felts do monstrous things over the years: torture unionizers, shoot miners without discretion, cast out whole families from their homes in the middle of winter.

Jude felt a deadening chill pass through his body. Florrie's terrified face and the blood streaming from her arm returned to Jude's mind. Her face morphed into Harvey's, white and taut with pain. Then, it was Willis, his face crumpled in agony, bruises blossoming on his jaw and brow. He reached for Jude, he wanted to hide behind Jude, he wanted Jude to protect him.

Jude swore under his breath, pressing the palms of his hands hard against his eyes to seal out the images. He needed sleep. If the Baldwins came, they came. If they mowed him down with their machine guns, what difference did it make? And the kid— well, Jude had gotten him this far. What happened to Harvey was out of his hands. For now, Jude would sleep.

Light filtered in through the cracked barn boards when Jude woke up. Sitting up, the urgency of their situation crashed back over him. He had not meant to sleep so long.

Jude remembered Harvey with a trickle of fear. Jude had slept in the horse's stall, and he moved to the other side. Harvey lay completely still on the ground, eyes closed. Jude could see the ghastly bloodstains on his shirt from the night before, but he could not tell what was old and what might be new. Jude fell to his knees beside Harvey and laid a hand on the boy's chest: it rose and fell weakly, and he could hear a small whistle of breath passing through his lips. Jude took his hand away and leaned against the stall, letting out a long breath.

Jude felt a twist of hunger in his belly, and he grudgingly stood back up and dug out a nub of jerky from Bradshaw's saddlebags. He sucked on the jerky for a few seconds to soften it, and the flavor of salt and smoke made his mouth water. Jude wandered to the front of the barn to look outside. He was beginning to wonder if there was, indeed, someone living in the cabin or if he had only imagined the light in the window last night. The only movement out in the yard was a couple chickens emerging drowsily from a copse of bushes.

He heard Harvey stir in the stall and call his name weakly. Jude moved away from the wall and returned to Harvey.

"You got any more water?" Harvey asked. He looked very pale, and shivers quaked his body.

"I'll get some," Jude replied.

The tenderness he had felt for the horse last night was gone, and now he regretted giving it the last of the water. Jude retrieved the canteen and returned to his lookout spot by the barn doors. He thought he saw a well out in the yard, but it was closer to the cabin than to the barn. Jude took several moments to weigh the risk of fetching more water.

His own mouth was dry and the salt from the jerky only served to make him thirstier. Jude crept to the back of the barn and eased through the doors. The air was icy-sharp and tingled over Jude's skin, but he felt invigorated after the stale atmosphere in the barn. Though the sun was rising, there were still enough deep shadows to make the venture seem less perilous. Jude moved quickly forward, pausing only a couple of times to glance at the road and the cabin for signs of movement. Besides the chickens, who gave him disinterested looks, nothing else stirred in the yard.

Jude came upon the well and pulled off the wooden cap, careful not to make a racket by dragging it across the stones. He glanced around once more, then grasped the crude pulley by the mouth of the well. As Jude worked the pulley, he could hear a bucket knocking around as it lowered into the well; a few moments later and he felt the rope tighten as the bucket filled with water, and Jude pulled faster to bring it up. Soon the sloshing bucket breached the mouth of the well, and Jude drew it up to rest on the stones, his eyes skimming the yard once more.

Though he knew it would be icy cold, Jude plunged his hand into the bucket and let his cupped palm fill with water. Jude tipped it into his mouth; the water tasted pure and green, the same as the scent of moss on river stones. He uncapped the canteen and pushed it down into the bucket, bubbles rising to the surface as the canteen filled with water. After stealing one last palm full of water, Jude screwed the lid back onto the canteen and glanced back up at the cabin in time to see a figure watching him from the window. Jude's heart tightened like a hiccough, and the person in the cabin fled from the window. Jude let the bucket plummet back into the well and sprinted to the barn.

"Harv! Get up!" Jude cried.

"What? Did they find us?" Harvey asked, sitting up with a wince.

"We've got to go," Jude said, thrusting the canteen into the horse's saddlebags and rushing to Harvey's stall. He bent down and wrapped his arm under Harvey's one shoulder and around his back, then in one hasty movement hauled upward. The blood rushed from Harvey's face and his knees buckled.

"Come on, Harv, stay with me, stay with me!" Jude cried, struggling under Harvey's dead weight. He considered striking Harvey's wound as he had before, but decided against it and instead swiped at Harvey's face with his free hand. Harvey's eyelids fluttered and he mumbled something, though his legs straightened beneath him.

"Atta boy, atta boy," Jude said. He dragged Harvey across the barn to the horse and pushed him awkwardly up into the saddle. As before, Harvey leaned forward onto the horse's neck as Jude lead the horse out of the stall and through the back doors. A voice hollered from the front side of the barn.

"Come on out! I seen you and know you're stowing in my barn."

It was an old man's quavering voice, and Jude felt the panic subside slightly. He hoisted himself quietly into the saddle behind Harvey, gripping the reins tightly.

"Alright, Harvey, we're going to make a run for it," Jude whispered. "Hold onto that saddle horn."

He could see Harvey's hands close around the saddle horn. He was breathing heavily, but still sitting halfway upright. Jude could hear the old man enter into the barn, and he kicked into the horse with a cry. The horse lunged forward, and Jude had to struggle as much to keep himself aright as he did to hold Harvey in place. They bolted through the yard with a skittering of pebbles and dust, the chickens flurrying back into the woods.

Chapter Seven

Harvey would not last long at this pace. Jude still felt exhilarated from their dash from the barn, but he could feel Harvey slumping in the saddle. He tightened his grip around Harvey's torso and slowed the horse. They had come a fair way down the mountain and were nearing the main road.

The sun had fully risen and a flock of blackbirds peppered the treetops, twittering noisily and flurrying from branch to branch. Jude felt relieved by their noise; descending the mountain, everything had been eerily quiet. Every crunch of the horse's hooves, every creak of the saddle seemed to cast deafening echoes through the hills.

"Jude," Harvey said feebly, "I don't know how much longer I can do this."

"Yeah," Jude murmured.

Jude remembered passing a small settlement when he and the other Baldwin-Felts trekked up the mountain several days ago. That seemed like years ago, but Jude recalled a run-down general store, a post office, and a few other buildings, plus the dumpy train station that the Baldwin-Felts had first arrived on. He would have to be careful; if the agents were waiting anywhere, it would be at the train station, but if Jude was lucky he might be able to pinch some supplies for him and Harvey.

They came upon a wide creek, and Jude remembered seeing a bridge across it at one point. He allowed the horse to follow the main road a bit farther until it came up to the creek, where Jude recognized the crude wooden bridge.

"Okay, kid," Jude said. "I've found a place for you to lie low."

The bridge was low to the ground as the creek was not very deep, but Jude could discern a space between the ground and the underbelly of the bridge that Harvey could fit under. Jude dismounted and peered under the bridge. He would be concerned about snakes and spiders if it weren't still so cold, so all he had to check for was adequate space for Harvey and ground that wasn't too wet. It was a tight angle between the bridge and the shore of the creek, but there was a sliver of cool, hard-packed clay near the top. Jude straightened and returned to the horse.

"Get down, if you can," Jude said.

Harvey grunted and slung his leg over the side of the horse, then more or less slid his way down to the ground. Jude caught him about his shoulder and led him to the bridge.

"Under here. You can rest some without nobody seeing you," Jude said.

"Where are you going?" Harvey asked with a wince, lowering to his knees to crawl painfully under the bridge.

"There's a town nearby. I'll go scout it out and see if I can't find us some supplies. Maybe even a way out of here. Scoot in close under there," Jude instructed, pointing to the base of the bridge.

Harvey inched as tight against the base of the bridge as he could. He looked awkward and uncomfortable, but he made no complaint.

"What are you going to do with the horse?" Harvey asked.

Jude turned to the horse. He could not take the horse into town as it would draw too much attention, but neither could he leave it here with Harvey in case someone saw it and began snooping.

"I haven't figured that out yet," Jude mumbled.

Harvey rested his head on the ground and closed his eyes. "Whatever you do, take the saddle off him. Thing's been on him for two days straight now."

Jude shook his head. "We've got to be able to dash if we need to," he said. "It's hard enough keeping you up with the horn to hold on to. We wouldn't last barebacked."

"Look," Harvey said, his voice weak but his eyes now opened and staring at Jude. "If you can't treat an animal right, you don't deserve to own it. That horse's been carrying two men nonstop since yesterday. Take off its gear."

"Fine. Whatever you say." Jude knew Harvey was right, but his nerves were frayed. "You stay here with your pony and let the Baldwins find you sitting pretty while I go risk my hide for some food and medicine."

Jude crawled out from under the bridge and went to the horse, roughly loosening the saddle belts and, with a grunt, lifting the saddle off the horse. His wounded arm throbbed with the strain, and Jude let the saddle drop irreverently to the ground.

Rather than shying sidewise, the horse drew closer to Jude. The hide on its back shivered visibly, and the horse thrust its head forward to have the bridle removed. Jude obliged, this time less crossly, and slid the saddle blanket off the horse's back. Freed of its gear, the horse lumbered to the creek and drank deeply. Jude dragged the equipment under the bridge and tossed the blanket onto Harvey.

"Enjoy the smell," he said.

Harvey wordlessly pulled the blanket over himself, his face strained.

"I'm going to find some food and something for you shoulder," Jude said.

"Wait till it's dark," Harvey mumbled. He was shivering again, with sweat on his brow.

"We can't wait that long," Jude said.

Jude diverged from the main road when he made his way to the town. March in the Blue Ridge Mountains was closer to winter than spring, and though sprigs of hardy greenery peeked out here and there, Jude wished for more coverage. Rhododendron and mountain laurel remained green year-round, but for the most part, he felt exposed as he moved through the bare forest.

The land began to flatten some as Jude drew closer to the town. He could see a break in the treetops where the railroad carved through, and Jude spotted small cabins tucked into the woods several acres away. Before long, Jude could see the dusty clearing that made up the mountain settlement. It was far enough into the morning now that several people milled around the buildings on different errands. Jude dropped to his stomach and crawled closer to the edge of town through the underbrush. He settled by a cluster of fir saplings and scanned the town more carefully.

Accurate to his memory, the only buildings in the settlement were a narrow general store, a very small post office, the train depot, and a duplex with two shingles nailed to the front reading DOCTOR and ROOM FOR RENT. A few people idled outside the general store, but Jude soon saw that the majority of the people— who he had taken for townsfolk—were Baldwin-Felts. They loitered by the train station, rifles in hand. The other residents cast anxious looks toward them and hurried past with their parcels.

Jude's heart hammered inside his chest. He had expected the Baldwin-Felts to be stationed at the train, but seeing them clustered by the depot sent fresh waves of fear through him. Jude eyed the distance between his position and the general store, though he already knew there was no chance for him to enter the store without the agents spotting him. Even if Jude chose to steal in through the back, there was not enough cover to conceal him.

Now unwilling to move for fear that the Baldwin-Felts might spot him, Jude remained where he was and tried to make out which of the Baldwin-Felts were by the station. Though he couldn't make out faces, he could tell quickly that Bradshaw was not among the agents—or, if he was nearby, he must be taking shelter or treatment with the doctor. There were four agents milling at the station, and Jude thought he saw one or two more through the windows of the general store. One exited the store, and Jude immediately recognized Johnny Prince's tight black curls, shiny with oil. His arm was tucked into a sling, but his free arm swung lazily by his side, the hand casually reaching up to rest on his holster.

Jude turned his eyes away from Prince and concentrated on the train station. The station was made up of a wooden platform and a squat brick building with one bench outside. There was a schedule board outside the building, but Jude could not make out any of the words. Stowing away on the train would be the best bet for him and Harvey, but it was clear that they had no chance of passing undetected by the Baldwin-Felts. Collecting supplies from the general store was equally impossible, and with stewing frustration Jude realized he could do nothing here.

It took close to an hour for Jude to clear himself from sight of the settlement. He likely could have gotten away faster, but the sight of the Baldwin-Felts—particularly Prince—had elevated Jude's sense of caution to the point where he was only willing to crawl painstakingly on his stomach till out of sight. After cresting a hill so that the settlement dropped from his vision, Jude rose to his feet, arching his back and shaking his legs, which were both aching.

For a brief moment, Jude felt a flash of resentment toward Harvey. Without the boy, Jude could easily stake out further down the train tracks and jump aboard out of sight of the Baldwin-Felts. But the resentment fizzled out quicker than Jude would have liked, and at that moment he felt twice as weary. He did not want to think long about Harvey. Jude remembered his pocketknife and bit of wood in his pocket and drew these out. He knew he should stay alert, watching the road and looking out for Baldwin-Felts, but instead he kept his head bent and whittled at the wood as he walked. Jude listened to the rhythmic crunching of his own boots, concentrating on making controlled, small strokes.

Jude made his way back to the bridge. He had stumbled upon a cabin on his way back, and watched from a distance for a few minutes as a woman and her two children chopped at the frozen ground in the garden with their hoes. He did not find it difficult to slip into the back of the cabin, pilfering a couple pieces of cornbread and rifling through the dusty medicine cabinet. He left his half-finished carving of the hare on the kitchen table in a weak effort to assuage his conscience. The bottle of iodine and thin roll of bandages he had found helped replace the guilt with relief.

Jude made himself eat the cornbread slowly as he walked. It must have been baked only that morning or the night before, for it had not yet turned dry and crumbly. Jude salivated heavily as he savored the buttery taste, and though he was still hungry after finishing, he felt heartened by the food.

The courage quickly went out of him as he approached the bridge and saw Harvey sprawled on his stomach several yards away from his hiding spot. Jude broke into a run, seeing no one else around.

"What happened?" Jude asked, skidding to a stop next to Harvey and dropping to his knees. He turned the boy over, and for a split second feared him dead, for the shoulder was wet with blood once more and Harvey's face was whiter than ever. But his eyes opened weakly and focused with difficulty on Jude's face.

"Horse began to drift," Harvey said, his voice barely audible. "I tried to get him to come back."

"A load of good it did you! Now you've lost the horse and half killed yourself, not to mention put yourself out in the open," Jude retorted. "Come on, we got to get you back."

"Jude—"

"Take this," Jude interrupted, shoving the second square of cornbread into Harvey's limp hand. "Eat it."

"Jude," Harvey repeated.

"What?"

"The Baldwins passed by earlier," Harvey said.

Jude stopped, his heart hammering. "When?" he asked.

"You had been gone about an hour," Harvey said. His hand closed around the cornbread, but he did not lift it to his mouth to eat. "Was a couple of them. They crossed the bridge, and I heard them talking about us."

"Glad to hear we're still remembered by our friends," Jude said. He was more preoccupied with getting Harvey out of the open and back under the bridge. "Come on, Harv, sit up for me. We got to get you moved."

"I heard them say something about the train station."

"Yeah, it's crawling with them," Jude said. Harvey made no effort to lift himself off the ground, and Jude wondered now if the boy even had the ability to move any further. "Kid, can't you sit up at all?"

Harvey laughed softly, closing his eyes. "It took me near an hour just to get this far. But listen, Jude—"

Jude sized up Harvey, wondering if he would be able to lift him up on his own. Harvey was a big boy, probably weighed even more than Jude. Jude ran his arm under Harvey's shoulders and helped him lift up. Harvey gasped, his good arm shooting out and gripping Jude's shoulder.

"Jesus!"

Jude flicked aside Harvey's shirt collar and peered at his shoulder. The bandana was wet with blood, and Jude felt a sickening dread pass through him. The wound needed treatment, badly. He had already waited too long.

"We've got to get you to a doctor," Jude murmured. He pushed the heel of his hand hard against Harvey's wound to stem the blood, and the boy ground his teeth to keep from crying out.

"I've been trying to tell you," Harvey grunted, his eyes pinched tightly shut. "Those Baldwins said something about a high warrant posted on us. Bradshaw's hot as a steamer about what we did—especially you."

Jude laughed grimly. He kept his arm firm behind Harvey's back, and the boy leaned heavily on him. "Doesn't matter. We gotta get you fixed up."

"There ain't no doctor who'd risk his neck to treat me. Not without turning us in," Harvey said.

Jude said nothing, his thoughts beginning to eddy. Harvey was right, of course. Once he had returned Harvey to his hiding spot—then what? He had already found that there was no solace in town, or even an opportunity to steal more supplies. Jude remembered the bandages and iodine in his pocket, but how long would those supplies last? Until the bullet was removed from Harvey's shoulder, the boy's wound would struggle to heal. Already, he was weak—weaker than Jude liked to admit.

He looked at the boy and noted how young he seemed. Jude guessed he could not be older than eighteen or nineteen, and thought back several years to when he was that age. At that point, he was already with the Baldwin-Felts running raids, and had shot multiple men. As he thought of this young version of himself, Jude recalled suddenly the image of Harvey at the raid, tugging the pig out of the burning shack with one arm, holding a half-dead chicken in the other.

There was no point in lying low and hiding. The Baldwin-Felts would eventually broaden their search and come upon them, and by that point Harvey would be even worse off, if not dead. Their only option was to leave these mountains, and Jude could see no other way out than by train.

Chapter Eight

Jude's thoughts darted nervously. He would have to get Harvey close to the settlement somehow, and wait to hear the train schedule. Where the train went, he did not care, just as long as it took them away from the Baldwin-Felts. Jude wished sorely that the horse had not wandered off, because he knew now that Harvey would not make it long on foot.

"Let's get this over with," Harvey said, looking ahead to the bridge. "It's getting late in the day."

"There's no point to hiding anymore," Jude said. "We've got to get that shoulder treated, and the Baldwins will find us sooner or later if we stick around here."

"What are you saying?"

"I'm saying we've got to catch a train out of here."

Harvey closed his eyes and laid a hand gingerly on his wounded shoulder with a frown. "Let me know when you've got a real plan set up," he said.

"This is the real plan," Jude snapped. "And it's the only one we've got."

With some help, Harvey could rise to his feet and the pair managed to stumble away from the bridge and settle farther down the creek, hiding in a thicket of mountain laurel. The leaf litter was flattened and soft underneath the shrub where deer had taken shelter, and after Jude ran back to the bridge to retrieve the saddle blanket, Harvey was soon made halfway comfortable. As dusk approached, Jude took advantage of the last rays of sunlight and took another look at Harvey's shoulder. Pulling away the soaked bandana, he was disgusted by what he saw.

Whether the wound had grown worse or he had simply not seen it clearly upon first inspection, Jude could not tell, but regardless it looked bad off now. The flesh around the bullet hole was white and rubbery-looking, and thick pus mingled with blood at the opening. The skin surrounding the wound was maroon and irritated, and Jude caught a curdling odor rising from the shoulder. Swallowing his nausea, Jude pulled the bottle of iodine from his pocket and dashed it upon the wound. Jude took the roll of bandages out next and wrapped the shoulder.

Jude made Harvey eat the square of cornbread, and the small bit of food seemed to revive him some. They both took a generous drink of water from the canteen before settling into the leaf litter, bracing themselves for the cold night that was about to come. Jude hoped Harvey would sleep for a few hours, but he himself planned to stay awake and work out the details of his scheme. He decided that they would need to be on the move before dawn in order to get close to the settlement without being seen. The Baldwin-Felts would likely still have a few men stationed as lookouts, but Jude would at least be able to find a hiding place from which to survey the settlement and work out the next steps.

Harvey did sleep deeply for a couple of hours, but as soon as the deep chill began to settle in the cove, his own shivering woke him up. Jude waited another hour to see if he would be able to fall asleep once more, but when he did not, he began to collect their few supplies.

"We might as well begin," Jude said. "We'll only be waiting to freeze if we stay here."

Harvey nodded, but Jude could not make out his expression in the dark. It was a moonless night, which he was thankful for, though he wondered once more how Harvey would manage the hike to the settlement.

The pair crawled out from under the mountain laurel. Harvey was able to stand upright, but they moved at a slow and careful pace, especially since the darkness concealed uneven ground and small rocks that tripped their feet. Jude found a fallen limb on their way and handed it to Harvey as a walking stick, but that provided only small stability.

The distance to the settlement seemed twice as vast in the dark, and on more than one occasion Jude wondered if he were leading them in the right direction. Now and then they would catch glimpses of the road, which reassured Jude, but they were not quite bold enough to follow it directly. The land was steep at several points, and they had to stop altogether as Harvey quickly grew lightheaded. Afraid he had pushed too hard, Jude allowed them both to rest for half an hour, though with his body stationary, his thoughts stirred.

Jude found himself frightened by his own plan, wondering what had driven him to abandon their hiding place and weaken Harvey with a strenuous hike. But seeing Harvey resting against a tree trunk, eyes closed and breathing slowly, Jude could not bring himself to break the boy's confidence in him. Reckless as the plan was, he would move forward with it and at least make an effort to escape.

After persuading a few more drinks of water into Harvey, Jude urged him to his feet again. Harvey rose wearily and leaned on the walking stick heavily. They continued for a little while, and though the land flattened some, Harvey's breathing remained heavy and labored.

The night was so dark that Jude did not at first realize when they neared the settlement. When the buildings began to take shape, Jude felt relief wash over him, and he tapped Harvey's arm.

"We're here," he whispered.

Harvey said nothing, but leaned on the walking stick. Jude moved to find a place for them to hide. There was a half-rotten stack of firewood behind the post office where several furry shrubs grew. It was closer to the settlement than Jude would have liked, but he could spy no other alternatives. He led Harvey down closer to the town, careful that they did not shuffle in the leaves and make noise.

An eye of light glowed in the center of town as a pair of lamps had been lit by the train station. Two Baldwins, bundled thickly in coats and looking unhappy to be out in the cold, kept guard by the train station. The brims of their hats were pulled so far down, and their scarves tugged so far up their faces, that only a little white strip by their eyes were exposed.

Jude left Harvey to slump against the wood pile as he skirted around the edge of the forest, drawing nearer to the station. The Baldwin-Felts did not speak to each other, but merely stamped their feet or clapped their frozen hands occasionally. The railway behind them appeared black and shiny as jet in the starlight, and it ran like a molten river around the bend of the land. The areas near to the tracks were cleared of trees and brush, and Jude could make out no place close to the tracks to hide in before jumping aboard the train. Anxiety mounting, Jude cautiously returned to the woodpile. A train would likely arrive sometime early in the morning, but they would have no chance to stow aboard with the Baldwin-Felts directly on the station.

If they could wander a bit up the track, however, then maybe there would be a chance to jump a car while the train slowed to the station. With the region being so hilly, the locomotive wouldn't be going very fast to begin with. Jude nodded, trying to convince himself that such an idea was possible.

Before dawn broke over the hills, Jude and Harvey managed to draw soundlessly away from the settlement and find a place to hide further up the tracks. Tall patches of grass, gray and brittle from a harsh mountain winter, carpeted the trenches on either side of the tracks. Jude placed Harvey in the middle of these grasses before traveling farther down the tracks himself. His plan was to hop a cart and slide open the door, by which time he hoped the train would have pulled close to Harvey's spot, and the boy could jump aboard with minimal exertion. That was the plan, though Jude knew there was little possibility of it succeeding, at least not with the ease he imagined.

Jude burrowed himself into another cluster of dry grass, the stalks sticking him like skewers. He glanced occasionally up the track at Harvey, who was nothing more than a dark speck barely visible in his own clump of grass. Farther up the track, on the opposite side, Jude could just make out the station with the Baldwin-Felts idling on the platform. Jude crossed his arms over his chest, allowing himself to catnap, assured that the train would wake him up.

Within an hour's time, just as the sky began to purple with dawn, Jude stirred awake as he imagined feeling, rather than hearing, the train approach. He drew himself to his hands and knees, but kept low to the ground. He felt the slightest of tremors move from the dirt up through the pads of his fingers, and a few seconds later could hear a faint rhythmic noise traveling up the tracks. Jude glanced down the other direction, but could not tell if Harvey was asleep or awake.

Jude wished now he had devoted more thought to what would happen if they failed to board the train; or, what he would do if he successfully boarded but Harvey could not manage to join. Pushing this last thought from his mind, Jude assured himself again that his plan was possible. It had to be.

At that moment the train surged into view, pulling around the corner and letting out a splitting whistle. From the corner of his eye, Jude saw Harvey bolt upward in his grass patch before quickly dropping down again. The Baldwin-Felts stirred on the station far down the track, and Jude felt his heart hammer. He could tell that the train was slowing, but it still moved fast along the sleek tracks. Jude kept his eyes locked on the carts farther back, telling himself over and over that it would slow, it would slow.

The train was close now, and Jude could make out the conductor through the window, stepping over and pulling the whistle once more. The whistle's deafening shriek made Jude cover his ears this time, and the next second his hair was being ruffled as the engine sped past. The moment the engine had passed, Jude rose to his feet, bent at the waist. He was braced with courage as he could now actually discern the train slowing, and he fixed his eyes on the third to last cart. It had a sliding door, and Jude marked it as the cart he would hop.

Jude did not bother to glance again at Harvey; he could not afford to be distracted. Harvey was on his own for now. The cart was close to Jude, and with his mind frenzying, he reached up for the lever on the door, high above his head. His hands managed to grasp it, but the train continued to move at a speed that kept Jude nearly sprinting to keep up. Now puffing like the engine, Jude bunched up his muscles and, with one massive effort, pulled himself up so that his feet scrambled upon the thin ledge at the bottom of the sliding door. His body arced out for a moment and Jude felt sure he would lose his balance and tumble off, but in the next moment he had mastered himself. He clung to the side of the cart for a second, halfway between exhilaration and terror.

Jude tugged at the lever on the door. It did not budge at first, as the wind sliding down the sides of the carts fought his efforts to push open the door. The train continued to slow, this time with an audible screech of the brakes, and Jude gave the lever another yank down and pushed against it with all the strength he could muster. A small opening appeared, and then all at once the door rolled back as the brakes were applied more heavily, and Jude nearly lurched off the cart. He thrust his weight sideways and landed inside the cart instead, heart thudding.

Scrambling back to the side on his hands and knees, Jude peered outside and saw that Harvey was only a cart or two away. The boy was standing now, since the train blocked them from view of the station. Not daring to yell, Jude held out his arms, and the next second Harvey was grasping at his elbows. There was no strength in Harvey's wounded arm, and Jude could not pull him aboard at first. Harvey began jogging to keep up, the blood quickly draining from his face.

"Come on," Jude grunted. "One—two—three!"

With a collective groan, Harvey leapt and Jude heaved, and then Harvey was clinging to the cart with his legs still dangling off. The train slowed drastically, and Jude felt then the urgency to hide themselves in the cart before it halted and others began to wander around the carts. With another grunt, he tugged Harvey onto the cart, and the boy laid on his back, chest heaving.

"Come on, come on," Jude urged.

He went back to the door and closed it with a yank. The cart was very dim, and there seemed to be nothing but wooden crates and sacks of grain—crowded, but with good places to hide.

Harvey did not respond to Jude's urging, so Jude scooped him up under his arms and dragged him irreverently toward the back of the cart. He found a cluster of heavy-looking barrels and wedged Harvey between a few while he nestled himself nearby. Instead of a rush of triumph at boarding the train, a sense of dread pressed on Jude as he realized boarding successfully was only half the key to escape.

A few moments later and the train came to a full stop, and

Jude could hear men's voices beginning to murmur outside. It sounded as though they were opening carts up closer to the engine. Jude reached over and prodded Harvey, though the boy did not move or speak. Jude whispered his name and crawled closer; Harvey's head rested on his chest and he appeared unconscious. For the moment, Jude felt relieved rather than concerned.

Without warning, the door to their cart rolled back, and Jude froze. He peered through the maze of crates and sacks, just barely discerning the black silhouettes of two men in the doorway of the cart. One heaved up onto the cart with a grunt while the other one remained on the ground, looking down at a clipboard.

"My mistake. Nothing in this one. There's lumber in the last cart; that goes. Get some men to unload," said the man with the clipboard.

The other man leapt back down and disappeared. The clipboard man absently reached up to close the door again when a third man appeared and glanced into the cart.

"Any sign of your men?" asked the man, still looking down at his clipboard.

Jude heard another man hoist himself into the cart, and the reek of Johnny Prince filled the cart. Jude shoved his fist under his nose to keep his rapid breathing from being heard. He heard footsteps roving the cart. There was a pause.

"No sign here," Prince said. The sobriety in his voice gripped Jude in fear. For as long as he had known Prince, he always spoke with swagger, sarcasm, or that manic energy that made him seem rabid. Never had he heard Prince speak with that flat, metallic coldness—the same hard resolve that came over Bradshaw's voice when he was furious. Prince strode back to the mouth of the cart and closed the door with his good arm, and Jude could hear his muffled voice from the outside.

"It's just a matter of time, though," Prince said. "I'll find them. And I'll flay them open like fish when I do."

The crunch of their boots on the gravel faded away, and Jude closed his eyes, resting his head back against the side of a barrel.

Chapter Nine

The train carried no passengers—at least, it had no passenger cart—and so it pulled out of the station within half an hour of arriving. Those thirty minutes passed with agonizing slowness for Jude, who expected at any moment for a workman or agent to reopen their cart door and find them hiding in the back. Besides the lumber mentioned earlier, however, it seemed that nothing else was unloaded at the small mountain settlement, and before long the conductors were preparing to leave once more. Where their ultimate destination was, Jude neither knew nor cared.

A shudder ran through the carts as the engine began to inch forward, and Jude felt a flood of relief so intense it made him almost nauseous. His head throbbed from the lack of sleep and good food over the past few days. Everything from Jude's muscles to his mind felt wrung-out like a kitchen rag, and his stomach clenched unpleasantly.

Harvey remained very still beside him, though he stirred slightly when the train resumed movement. His condition heightened Jude's anxiety, and he began to wonder if there were possibly any supplies stored in their cart that might be of some use. Jude rose to his feet, taking a moment to steady himself as the cart wobbled some with the accelerating speed of the train. The inside of the cart was dark, and Jude could do little better than grope around the barrels and sacks. Some of the crates could not be opened at all without a crowbar, or the sacks without splitting the tops with a knife, though here and there Jude found a trunk or barrel with a loose lid that allowed him to rifle inside. This offered little encouragement, though, as one contained nothing but seed packets, and the other was only bolts of cotton broadcloth.

Jude made his way back and found Harvey awake, gingerly pulling himself up to lean against the nearest barrel.

"So we made it," Harvey said.

"Of course we did," Jude replied. His eyes scanned over the cart, anxious to find something useful.

"Got any food?"

"That's what I'm looking for, isn't it?"

Jude struggled with the lid of a nearby barrel, avoiding Harvey's pained eyes. Having pried the lid off the barrel, Jude found ceramic cups and stacked plates, but he continued to rifle through the straw packing. Reaching deeper into the barrel, his hand grazed cool glass, and his fingers soon closed around the neck of a bottle. Jude's stomach gave a little flip as he carefully pulled up the bottle, the top plugged with a cork and full of liquid. Scarcely was the bottle out of the barrel then Jude had wrenched out the cork and taken a swig that scorched his mouth and throat.

"Hot damn!" He took another burning, brilliant gulp.

"What?" Harvey asked in a startled voice.

"We just found ourselves some cola," Jude said, wiping his mouth with his sleeve. He lifted the bottle up for Harvey to see, giving it a little shake.

"How'd that get in here?"

"Bootleggers," Jude said before taking another swig.

"Someone'll be picking it up, then, won't they?"

"Sure. We'll leave them some pretty bottles to play with."

Harvey sighed, resting his head back against the barrel. "All I want is food."

"This is the best thing we could have found in here," Jude said. "For you and me both."

"How do you mean?"

Jude held the bottle up close to his mouth, looking at Harvey's shoulder. His stomach was already churning. "We're going to get that bullet out."

Harvey scowled, moving a hand over his wound. "You've lost your head."

"With the help of our friend here, we can do it," Jude said, and thrust the bottle into Harvey's hand.

"It's dark as pitch in here. You couldn't see well enough even if I let you try."

Already the alcohol warmed Jude through, easing the aches in his body and renewing his courage. "There'll be a lantern in here somewhere," he said. "They've got to be able to see when they take inventory, haven't they?"

He rose to his feet and stumbled around the perimeter of the cart, calling over his shoulder: "Take a taste of that stuff!"

Jude heard Harvey scoff, but an outburst of coughing a few seconds later confirmed that Harvey had taken his suggestion. Before long, Jude had made his way to the opposite side of the cart where, true to his guess, he found a lantern attached to the wall of the cart, a packet of matches tucked carelessly inside. Jude pulled out the matches, lit one, and pocketed the rest. The entire cart flared with sudden visibility as the match met the oil, and Jude closed the door of the lantern. Wary of the jostling train, Jude made his way back to Harvey.

"You're nuts if you think I'll let you work on my shoulder," Harvey said, and Jude noticed a thin outbreak of sweat on the boy's forehead. Jude felt little sympathy now; he was sick of worrying about the shoulder, and whatever liquid was inside the bottle gave him a dangerous blaze of courage.

"Take some more medicine like a good boy," Jude said, picking up the bottle and pushing it to Harvey's mouth. Sputtering, Harvey took a couple swigs before thrusting it away with disgust.

"Enough!" he shouted, some of the alcohol spilling down his chin.

"You'll do as I say," Jude said, pushing his finger into Harvey's face. "I'll be damned if we don't get that bullet out. Give me the bottle."

"Like hell," Harvey said, clutching it to his chest. "You've lost your head with what you've already had."

Jude yanked the bottle out of Harvey's hand with ease. He took a swig and wiped his mouth with his sleeve. "Shut up. We're getting that bullet out, whether you like it or not. We've only got till the train pulls into the next station, and God knows where that is."

Whether out of sudden weariness or a recognition that he would be unable to overpower Jude, Harvey dropped his fight. "All right," he said, looking pale once more. "But don't drink any more. It'll be hard enough with the train moving without you having shaky hands."

"It's a deal," Jude said, though he snuck in another sip. He wasn't sure what kind of alcohol was in the bottle, but it was strong. "Here. You do the rest of the drinking for me. It'll cut the pain."

Jude propped the lantern on the floor beside them and helped Harvey pull his arm out of his sleeve. Jude began to unwrap the bandage, and Harvey took a generous swig of liquor. The wound underneath had taken on a watery brownish tinge from the iodine, but there was still an angry expanse of red spreading from the mouth of the wound. Jude felt queasy looking directly at the hole, which was tattered, white in some places and blood-crusted in others. Jude recognized once again that he had no utensils with which to extract the bullet. With a sudden grim idea, he stood and returned to the barrel where he had found the bottle of hooch.

Rifling through the straw and ceramics, by some chance Jude found what he searched for. Wrapped in a napkin was a bundle of silverware: a few butter knives, tablespoons and sugar spoons, and forks. Jude returned to Harvey's side with the bundle and one plate and took the bottle from the boy's hand without speaking. Soaking the napkin in the alcohol, he began to wipe the silverware piece by piece before laying them onto the plate. Harvey watched without speaking.

"Alright," Jude said when he had finished.

"Give me something to hold on to," Harvey said quickly.

Jude took Harvey's shirt and crumpled it into a ball. "Here," he said, pushing it into the boy's hand.

Harvey gripped the shirt and nodded. The boy quivered visibly from head to toe.

"We're getting this bullet out."

"Just start."

Starting was the trouble. Jude breathed deeply, and after a moment, his hand lifted the sugar spoon from the plate. He pushed its rounded back lightly against the opening of the wound. A hiss of pain escaped from Harvey, and his eyes pinched shut. Jude paused, judging the size of the sugar spoon against the size of the wound. Yes, it would fit—with some effort. Jude pushed the spoon in, scraping the wound in search of the bullet as one scoops marrow from a bone.

The twenty minutes that passed felt less like a hasty, gruesome extraction and more like a multiple-hour operation. By the end of it, though, the ceramic plate was streaked with blood where the utensils rested, and a little bullet rolled around the base of the plate. Harvey laid very still, drifting in and out of consciousness. His shoulder bled openly, though Jude had sloshed it with the liquor and more iodine and wrapped it in leftover gauze.

Jude sat slumped against a crate a few feet away with his back to Harvey. He cradled the bottle, now almost empty, and tried to ignore his own violent shaking. The cart seemed dim and cavernous, and the trundling of the train made the shadows flicker. There were moments when Jude thought he saw faces in the folds of the burlap sacks, or the whorls of wood grain on the barrels. He took another trembling swig from the bottle.

"Not so bad, was it, Harvey?" Jude called over. He could hear the tremulous slur at the end of his words. "Wasn't so bad," he mumbled to himself.

He had resumed guzzling the alcohol in the middle of the procedure. Harvey's bitten-off screams unnerved him. The sound of his cries opened memories Jude worked hard to keep locked away. Willis had cried like that when Pa beat him, or smeared cigarette butts into his wrists. Why had Jude never stopped him? Why did he do nothing to make it stop? But he couldn't stop as he worked on Harvey, even as the boy pleaded with him.

Jude heard Harvey exhale: a deep, shuddering sound, heavy with pain. All the old memories floated up inside his head, like dead fish rising to the surface. For a minute Harvey's face wasn't Harvey's, but Willis's. Jude cut off a cry of fear—the shape was Harvey again. He clutched the bottle and felt the fog of drunkenness start to envelop him. His body began to wrack as tears glazed his cheeks; he bit his own hand so that no sound escaped but dry, hoarse gasps.

"I'm sorry," Jude whispered in a mangled voice. "I'm sorry."

Passage of time was lost to him then; before long, he could barely distinguish between the barrels and Harvey's slumped shape, much less how long the train had been chugging along. When he had drained the first bottle of hooch, he rummaged through the barrel and found another. Jude sloshed some onto his own shoulder, unaware of what he was really doing, then drank more. He did not offer any to Harvey; he was unable to bring himself to even look in Harvey's direction anymore. He couldn't handle the tricks his mind was playing.

Every few minutes Jude spoke aloud to himself, though he forgot what he said as soon as he finished speaking. The rhythm of the train and the rocking of the cart was the only thing he found comfort in; the next moment, the alcohol overpowered him and he laid back, half unconscious. He would likely have remained that way for hours had he not been jolted awake by the opening of the cart door.

The train had stopped. Spikes of white light streamed through the opened door, and the brightness sent unbearable spasms of pain through Jude's head. He nearly barked a command to close the door, but a shred of consciousness reminded him of his situation and he said nothing, only passed his hands gingerly over his eyes. They would be discovered now, Jude felt, yet he found it hard to care. He made himself sit up slightly, propped against some object, still holding the bottle. Sour nausea was already brewing low in his gut.

"It'll be somewhere in there," said a voice from outside. "I'll get some men to help you."

"That won't be necessary," answered a man's voice.

"We'll just hop in and find it," came a third voice, this one with a Scottish accent. "Nothing but a couple barrels."

"Suit yourselves," said the first man. "Mind you don't tamper with the other cargo."

The cart jiggled as the men pulled themselves aboard. Jude could hazily make out their outlines in the light of the opening—one big man, one smaller and sleeker. Grudgingly, Jude turned his head to look at Harvey. He saw that Harvey's eyes were open and watching the men. Otherwise, he was completely still.

"This way," said one of the men, and their footsteps came toward Jude and Harvey. Jude closed his eyes. He heard the footsteps abruptly stop.

"What in heaven!" exclaimed the Scotsman.

Jude opened his eyes and found the pair standing a few feet away, surveying him and Harvey. The Scotsman was broad and middle-aged, with a bushy gray mustache and shirtsleeves rolled up to reveal thick, hairy forearms. The second man was a sharp contrast: young and well-groomed, dressed in a pinstripe suit.

"Just a pair of stowaways," said the young man dismissively.

The Scotsman gave them a sideways glance before moving to the nearby cargo, pausing over the pillaged barrel of ceramics and the hidden moonshine.

"Bishop!" he hissed.

Letting his eyes linger a moment on Harvey and Jude, the young man then turned to where the Scotsman stood. He looked into the barrel, but said nothing. They both turned back to Jude and Harvey, and the Scotsman snatched up the lantern and hovered it over them.

"Mary, Mother of God," he breathed, seeing Harvey's bloodied shirt.

Before Jude could react, the man named Bishop yanked the bottle of liquor from his arms. He held it up, surveying the empty space, and his eyes quickly found the other empty bottles rolling nearby.

"Go on and turn us over," Jude slurred, the sound of his own voice making his head ache. "We'll see what the cops make of this hooch we've come across."

Bishop and the Scotsman exchanged glances.

"Who are you?" Bishop asked.

"Don't see a reason to tell you."

The Scotsman's eyes fell to the floor and he let out a cry of disgust. "What've they done to Warby's silverware?" He knelt down, peering over the bloodied cutlery on the plate, his face crumpled with revulsion.

Bishop remained still, rolling the bottle of liquor slowly in his hands. "They'll have to come with us, Monty. No time for bickering."

Harvey said nothing, watching everything with expressionless eyes. Monty's eyes kept returning to the boy's shoulder.

"Alright lad," said Monty, laying a firm hand on Harvey's good shoulder. "Let's cooperate for a bit, eh? I'll help you, you help me?"

Jude felt a flare of panicked heat rush through his nerves, and he sat up. "Leave him alone!" he yelled.

Bishop knelt beside Jude, and their faces became level. He had very pale blue eyes, eyes that seemed calculating and cold.

"I wouldn't consider myself in any position to give orders, if I were you," Bishop said in a low voice. "Whatever's happened here we'll find out soon enough, but for now you'll keep your voice down and come quiet. You'll find that cops aren't the only way to get you in trouble around here."

Chapter Ten

Whitmill, South Carolina, 1922

Jude drifted in and out of consciousness, like a piece of wood bobbing on a surface of water before being pulled back down by a current. Harvey was at the back of the automobile, somewhere. Jude was wedged in between the one in the suit and the Scotsman called Monty. Bishop smelled like Listerine, and Monty smelled musty, like brown bread and old wool. Jude didn't mind the wool, but the yeasty smell turned his stomach and he retched into the other man's shoulder.

"If you can't hold your juice, you'll be strapped to the back like baggage," Monty said, while the other one—Bishop—shoved Jude away.

Jude's head rolled uncomfortably onto his own shoulder, but he found he couldn't move it. He sunk again into blackness.

When Jude rose back to the surface, the car was at a stop and everything was bright. Jude pinched his eyes till only a sliver of whiteness filtered through his lashes. He did not feel Bishop or Monty on either side of him. Jude slowly raised his eyelids and saw a skinny house in front of the car. There was a shallow porch at the front with a shabby railing, and strings of chimes hanging from the rafters.

The car wobbled and Jude grunted, twisting around to see Monty reaching into the back, lifting Harvey halfway up. Jude said dimly, "He can't move."

Monty's face was indistinct. He might have said something back, but Jude couldn't tell. Jude spoke up again: "Don't move him, he ain't well."

Jude saw Harvey glide off the leather seats and out of sight, like an oyster disappearing down a throat. Jude turned back to the front of the car. Bishop stood on the porch, and a girl was with him. Monty shuffled up, awkward with Harvey's big body in his arms.

"Hey," Jude mumbled. Then, louder: "Hey!"

Bishop glanced at the car, said something to the girl, and walked over. Flicking open the door, he leaned in. "You, too," he said.

"Not on your life," Jude slurred. His lips and chin felt wet.

"Out," Bishop commanded. He gripped Jude's arm and yanked him out. The world titled and Jude felt sick. Concentrating on keeping his mouth clamped shut, Jude allowed Bishop to steer him roughly toward the house.

"Lay him there," said the woman's voice. "Here—use this pillow behind his head."

Jude felt a rush of relief. He wanted nothing more than to lie down and sleep, but in the next moment he was shoved into a wooden chair. Jude grunted and his eyes flew open, only to find that it was Harvey, not him, being lowered gingerly onto a frayed chaise lounge. The girl he had seen on the porch leaned over him. Jude heard her gasp softly.

"Who is he? What's happened?" she asked. Kneeling beside the lounge, she turned to look at Bishop and Monty with eyes round as saucers. "Are either of you hurt?"

"No," said Bishop.

"What about him?" she asked, and Jude felt a pair of eyes fall on him.

"Pickled," Monty scoffed.

The girl turned back to Harvey and peeled back his shirt. "Sakes alive!"

"We found them on the train," Bishop said. "They drank as much of the hooch as they could, and then some. We'll be lucky if the loaders don't smell it spilled everywhere and come hunting us."

Jude sunk deeper into the chair, wishing the trio would stop talking.

"We don't know what happened to them," said Monty, gesturing to Harvey. "But Warby, I'm afraid your silver's been spoiled."

The girl called Warby was rustling in a nearby cabinet where Jude could see her better. She was a tall girl, with a narrow torso that broadened into fleshier hips and thighs that pushed just slightly against her skirt. She wore a bumpy cardigan and had a pair of rectangular glasses hanging from a strand of seed pearls around her neck. "What do you mean, silver?" she asked. She had a faint voice, as though she were used to speaking just above a whisper.

"The tableware Bishop ordered for you," Monty said, running a meaty paw over his face. "That sod was using it for meatball surgery, or some other tomfoolery, who knows—"

"You shouldn't have bothered yourself over that," said Warby, beginning to turn red. "I never asked you to order it for me."

"You never ask for anything in the first place," Bishop said.

Warby cleared her throat. "He's bled out badly," she said, pulling the shirt back over Harvey's shoulder. "Looks like the bullet's gone, though."

"Is it infected?" Bishop asked.

"Yes. He's got a fever that needs bringing down." Warby raised the glasses hanging around her neck and perched them on the tip of her nose as she again leaned over Harvey. All three of them had their backs turned to Jude now.

"I was shot too, you know," Jude said loudly.

Warby looked up at Bishop, who sighed. "Grazed him, at most," he explained. "Monty, see if you can sober this one up. I have some questions I want answered."

Monty walked over, and Jude quieted. "Please," he mumbled, not knowing what he was pleading for.

"On your feet," Monty said. "A dip in the Russy would do you some good."

Monty hauled Jude up by the scruff of his shirt, and the room swam.

"Get me outside," Jude said in a garbled voice, feeling the bile rise in his throat. Monty pushed him out the door, and they were scarcely off the porch before Jude hurled vomit onto the walkway. He heard Monty mutter a curse behind him before gripping his shoulder, keeping Jude from falling down into his own pool of vomit.

"Up, you," Monty said, giving Jude a few rough slaps on the back.

"Let me down," Jude panted. His head was roaring, and his stomach felt ready to squeeze out more poison.

"Up," Monty said again, gripping Jude under the armpit and jerking him up.

"Oh, God," Jude moaned. He could not remember being so sick, not since the early days after Willis died, when hooch was a new and dangerous medicine. He closed his eyes, though that provided sparse relief from the dizziness. He only opened his eyes when he heard the running water. Monty was pulling him toward a silty river, flowing sluggishly and lined with long grasses.

"Can you swim?" Monty asked, his voice seeming disembodied and far away.

Jude groaned.

"Right," Monty said. "Deep breath!"

Before Jude could object, he felt himself lifted off his feet and suddenly flung to the side, and he crashed into frosty-cold water. His mouth opened in shock and grassy-tasting water flooded in. Sharp feeling bloomed across Jude's skin as the intense cold hit him, and for a few minutes the throbbing in his head eased. For a dreamlike moment, the panic subsided and he felt relief, cradled by an invisible current.

Monty's hands clasped his shoulders and Jude was pulled back above the surface. He ached all over, this time from the breathtaking cold that seemed to gnaw the skin right off his body. His head began to throb again, though his vision was clearer. Monty pulled him back onto the shore, the long yellow grasses parting like hair.

"Now that's better, isn't it?" Monty asked, rubbing his hands on his trousers.

Jude knelt on the ground, his hands pressed into the overgrown grass. He spewed water away from his mouth, taking in deep gulps of air.

"Just leave us the hell alone," Jude said, staring at the ground and trying not to throw up again. "Ain't no reason for you to keep us here like this."

"You think so?" Monty said. "From where I'm standing, it looks to me as though you've stolen goods from us."

Jude groaned. "I didn't drink your damn hooch for a good time, don't you see? It was for the kid—I had to take care of the kid—"

"Aye, you have a real bedside manner, lad."

"You don't have any idea what we've been through."

"No, I don't. But that's why I threw you in the lake, see? You're sobering up already."

Jude raised his head to glower at Monty. Monty grabbed Jude by the scruff and heaved him to his feet before dragging him back to the house. "Come on," Monty said. "Let's hear this story of yours."

Chapter Eleven

The kitchen in the back of Warby's house was extremely small, made to feel even smaller with four people crammed around the narrow dining table pushed into the corner. Jude leaned heavily on the table, an old quilt wrapped around his shoulders, his eyes closed against the searing pain of the lamplight overhead.

Bishop pushed a mug across the table. "Coffee," he said. "Will you drink it?"

"Thanks," Jude said gruffly. The mug was hot, and the heat pressing into his palms sent a trickling sensation up his arms. He took a slurp, knowing it would burn his tongue, but not caring. Warby, who also sat at the table, watched him over her half-spectacles, the elderly mannerism at odds with her childlike features.

"Right," Monty said, slapping his palms down on the table, making Warby jump. "You should start by telling us your name, the name of the boy, and how you got here."

Jude took his time swallowing the coffee. His brain felt like a bowl of hot mash, and his churning stomach continued to distract him. He couldn't focus enough to decide whether it was smart to come clean with these people, or to spin a lie and bide some time. It occurred to him then that he wasn't even sure where they were. For all he knew, they could be one town over and Prince was on his way.

"My name's Jude Washer, the kid is Morgan, Harvey Morgan."

"How do you know each other?" Bishop asked.

Jude ran his thumb over the rim of the cup. He had to change the angle of this conversation to bide himself time to think. "Look," he said. "Let's do a little exchange. I tell you a little about me, you tell me a little about y'all."

"You're in no position to be calling the shots here," Monty growled.

Bishop was considering Jude with chill blue eyes. "Perhaps not," he said. "But some give-and-take could be productive. What do you want to know?"

"Well, for starters," Jude began, lifting up the mug for another gulp of coffee, "where the hell are we?"

"You're in Whitmill, South Carolina," Warby answered.

A smile stretched over Jude's face. "I'll be damned," he said.

"Our turn," Monty said. "How do you know the kid? Harvey?"

"We worked together," Jude answered.

"How'd you get shot?"

"My turn to ask."

Monty huffed and leaned back in his chair. "Twit," he muttered.

Jude turned to Bishop and smiled. Hungover as he was, he was beginning to feel some control returning to his side. They had more than left Virginia—they had followed the line of the Blue Ridge all the way down to South Carolina. With two whole states between him and Johnny Prince, he could breathe again. "So. Bootleggers. What's your setup?"

Warby slid her spectacles off her nose and stared at them folded in her hands. "We purchase alcohol from poor mountain people, then distribute their wares to other poor mountain people who can't seem to stop drinking it." Her eyes darted up to Bishop with an angry flare.

Monty cleared his throat, shifting in his seat. Bishop said, quietly, "Warby."

Color rose in Warby's cheeks. "You know it's true, Sidney. That, or we peddle it to rich politicians who throw secret debaucheries away from the cities. You both know how I feel about it, and it doesn't make much difference if he knows, either," she added, meeting Jude's eyes. "That boy in there—how many men have I patched up with gunshot wounds like that?"

Monty glared at Jude across the table. "Which brings me back to my original question."

Jude surveyed all three of their faces, trying to sum up the risks before him. He was sitting at a table with people who had seen as much violence as he had, from the sound of it. Jude craned his head to look into the front parlor, where he could just make out the shape of Harvey's feet overhanging Warby's couch. If these people had hid bootlegging and gunshots from the law, then they could hide them, too.

Clearing his throat, Jude leaned forward onto the table. "You ever heard of Baldwin-Felts down here before?"

Bishop frowned. "Yes, I see them in the papers. They don't have much reason to come down this south, though."

"Are you one of them?" Warby asked, looking twice as wary as before.

"I was," Jude answered. He flicked his thumb over his shoulder at Harvey. "So was he. A couple days ago we decided we didn't like how they were running their business, so the other Baldwin-Felts took to shooting us. We got out of there as best we could."

Jude hoped they wouldn't ask Harvey for his version of the story.

Bishop leaned back in his chair, crossing his arms over his chest. "Your colleagues shot you for trying to leave?"

"Well," Jude said, taking a gulp of coffee and wiping his mouth with his sleeve, "we were sort of in the middle of a raid."

"A great plan," Monty said.

"They came after us, and we hopped a train. Harvey was pretty bad off, and the bullet was stuck in his shoulder. I'll admit I don't know the most about first aid—"

"You could have sent him into shock," Warby shot across the table, glaring at Jude as she rubbed the lenses of her spectacles between the layers of her sweater.

"I found the liquor, and I did what I could to...well, you know." Jude's stomach was turning on him again. He changed the subject. "Next thing I know, you two were dragging us out of the car. And here we are."

"Here we are," Bishop muttered, studying his hands. They were quiet for a while, and Monty and Warby were watching Bishop. Jude drank his coffee, letting the silence stretch, anticipating a decision at the end of it.

"Is there a chance you were followed?" Bishop asked eventually.

"From two states down?" Jude asked. Prince's silhouette framed by the train car door reentered his mind. If Prince had seen them, or even suspected they were there, he would have captured them then, surely. There was a tingle of dread in Jude's stomach, though he knew he had no reason to fear Prince anymore. No use in expressing any of that to the bootleggers, though. "Hell no. The Baldwins are dogged, but they're not going to come all the way down here just to chase two rogue agents."

Bishop looked up and his eyes were steely, not unlike Bradshaw's military gaze. "I've heard of Baldwin-Felts being hired to enforce Prohibition. The local sheriffs don't mettle with us—some buy from us outright—and we've skirted the marshals that make their way up here every few years. But the Baldwin-Felts might just be a different caliber. So I'll ask again: are you sure nobody followed you?"

"Nobody followed us." Jude moistened his lips. "They'll think we're still in Virginia."

Bishop drummed his fingers on the table, staring at Jude. For half a second, Jude thought he would stand up and declare they weren't worth the risk. But then Bishop spoke again. "Alright. So now it comes down to this: you know our dirt, and we know yours. If it stayed at that, then we'd let you go on your way."

Jude could see the deal being laid out like a map on the table. He knew the rules to this game, and he was interested in playing. They needed a place to lie low, someplace where people wouldn't ask too many questions. This was turning into just the right opportunity, if he could play his cards right.

"But," Bishop resumed, "you have ruined a valuable portion of wares owned by our party. Do you have money to recompense?"

Jude didn't have any money, and he guessed Bishop already

knew that. They weren't really after money, then. They needed something else. "I don't have a dime on me, mac," he said.

"In that case, we will hold you accountable via labor, till the amount of lost merchandise is repaid or both parties are satisfied."

"Sidney—"

"Bishop—"

Monty and Warby exchanged glances as they protested at the same time. Bishop held up his palm. "You both know we're short on hands."

"There's a reason for that," Warby said, pushing away from the table and marching into the front room where Harvey laid.

Jude watched as Warby fussed over the blankets covering Harvey before turning to stare rigidly out the window. He faced Bishop again. "What about the kid? He won't be able to work for a while."

"Assuming he was not a willing participant in the debauchery on the train ride—"

"Listen, I explained—"

"...we will hold you accountable for his portion of dues," Bishop finished. "He may take the time to recover while you work, with the understanding that you are accountable for any expenses he accrues. Warby is more than capable of tending to his wounds during that time."

"Jesus knows she has the experience," Monty muttered. He looked sideways at Bishop, a frown sloping below his grizzled mustache.

"Do we have a deal?" Bishop asked.

"Hold your horses," Jude said. "What exactly will this work entail?"

"Traveling to our different vendors, buying liquor off them, and returning the wares to our warehouse for distribution. Sometimes we do deliveries, but most of our customers send someone to us to pick up the liquor. Every now and then, we'll get asked to collect special liquors for a party—"

"Debauch," Monty interrupted.

Bishop threw a sharp glance at Monty. "The shipment that you intercepted was one such delivery of specialty liquor. Cognac, actually. Which, coincidentally, we will have to replace. We get mostly whiskey and crude wines from our vendors here locally. Anything other than that is typically imported from elsewhere." Bishop spread his hands open on the table. "Any other questions?"

"Yeah," Jude said. He tipped his empty cup toward Bishop. "Got anything on you now?"

Bishop and Jude went out to the car waiting out front.

"Where are we going?" Jude asked. He didn't like the idea of leaving Harvey behind.

"There's one more member of our team you need to meet," Bishop answered. "He leads our river runs. You'll be quartering with him, and Harvey will, too, once he can be moved."

Monty stood on Warby's front porch, watching as they pulled away from the house. He was still frowning.

"He doesn't seem too keen on this deal we've struck," Jude said. "Neither does the dame."

Bishop sat with immaculate posture behind the wheel, steering with calm, fluid movements. "The bootlegging business has its wearying aspects," he said. "Monty and Warby have both felt that in recent times. But we need the help, and we're low on men. Very low on men."

Jude popped his knuckles absently. "Do I want to hear that story?"

Bishop switched gears with a jerk. "No."

Jude was tempted to persist, but decided to stay on Bishop's good side, at least for the first few days. Instead, he asked, "So, what's with the girl?"

"Who?" Bishop replied, staring ahead through the window.

"The one taking care of Harvey. Warby."

"Oh," Bishop said, glancing at Jude. "Miss Jefferson."

They were coming up alongside a broader portion of river, the same river Monty had thrown Jude in earlier.

"What's a girl like Warby doing with a crowd like yours?"

"You might say she was grafted in," Bishop replied. "We've all been at this for a while. Her father started the business."

Bishop pulled up the car along a series of long, shabby wooden docks that stretched into the belly of the river, with multiple boats bobbing nearby. They climbed out of the car. Jude ran his hands over the front of his trousers, which were still damp from the river—this same river. Bishop buttoned the top button of his jacket, straightened his sleeves, then strode toward the docks. "Warby's father was a doctor," Bishop explained, not looking to see if Jude followed. "Jefferson moved here with Warby after his wife died. By that time, he had obtained a license from the government to prescribe medicinal alcohol." Bishop's eyes flicked sideways at Jude. "You can deduce the rest, I imagine," he said. "He was an important member of our network for many years. He more or less trained Warby as a nurse over his lifetime."

Their shoes suddenly hit the dock planks with rhythmic thumps, and nervousness bobbed inside Jude's throat as he realized he was out in the open for the first time since they left the

Baldwins. Beside him, Bishop continued walking with a cool, measured stride.

"Did he die or something?" Jude asked. He reminded himself of the two states between him and Johnny Prince, exhaling slowly out his mouth. Everything was fine.

Bishop was quiet for several paces. "Yes, he did," he answered. "In a feud with some rival bootleggers."

Jude opened his mouth to ask another question, but Bishop interrupted: "We're here."

They stood before a small riverboat. It was painted an inconspicuous brown, with a steam stack rising in the middle of the deck. The deck area was scarcely more than a walkway surrounding the pilothouse, with a flimsy metal awning over the back portion of the boat. Jude could see two small portholes—nickel-sized, they seemed to him—in the hull of the boat. At the prow, "Damselfly" was stamped in simple white letters.

Bishop came alongside the Damselfly and paused, his fingers working to unbutton his coat. Then, with catlike agility, he jumped the short gap between dock and boat. The next instant and he was upright and sleek as a metal rod, fussing at the lines of his suit. Jude scoffed and hopped aboard, his swagger faltering for a moment as he felt the boat bobbing under his feet. Bishop gave him a silent, withering look before opening the door leading below deck.

"Lebo?" Bishop called down, setting his foot onto the first step.

"Who's there?" came a voice from below, in a heavy nasal accent.

"Sidney," Bishop replied, beginning to descend the staircase. He threw an arm behind him and gestured for Jude to follow. "I've brought you a new recruit."

Jude ducked his head as he descended the shallow stairs, and he heard a cackle ripple through the cabin.

"Haw, now," came the voice. "Let's see this poor son of a bitch."

Chapter Twelve

The cabin of the little riverboat was dark and narrow. With the light from the tiny portholes, Jude could just make out a rickety table surrounded by mismatched chairs, and a few cabinets built into the walls. A dusty sofa, holes torn into its upholstery, was crammed into one corner, and it was on this piece of furniture that the speaker lay sprawled. He was a remarkably thin man, wearing a raggedy sweater with the neckline stretched out, revealing protruding collarbones. Though his face was relatively young, he had a starkly receding hairline, and his wide grin showed several missing teeth.

"Been waiting to hear from you, Sid." He unfolded himself from the couch and clasped hands with Bishop.

"Staying out of trouble, I hope," Bishop said.

"About as well as I can," said the man. There was a slight sibilance to his voice as his words whistled through the gaps in his teeth.

"Lebo, I've got a new recruit for you," Bishop said again, turning to face Jude. "Jude Washer. Jude, this is Lebo Edson. He runs orders for us up and down the river."

"I'm a water-bug, is what he means," Lebo said, grinning and extending his hand. It was surprisingly big and hairy-knuckled, like a long-fingered paw at the end of Lebo's thin arm. "About never get off the old Russy, as much work as we've been doing lately," Lebo said.

"You're about to get more," Bishop said. "The order fell through."

Lebo's face screwed up. "Haw, now. What happened?"

Jude met Bishop's eyes for a split second before Bishop answered, "Rough handling at the trains. Busted up the whole order. We were lucky to get the crates off before anyone smelled it."

Jude crossed his arms over his chest, studying Bishop's face for a giveaway. He wasn't a half-bad liar.

"Hell," Lebo said, running his giant hand over his face. "Took you a week to track down that supply."

Bishop fiddled with his shirt cuffs, masking a spasm of annoyance on his face. "Regardless," he said, "we have to make up for the lost inventory. I'll have to follow on some leads I've been avoiding—Teague territory."

Lebo looked off to the side, hands on his hips. "Well—we'll do what we have to, Sid."

"I've brought on Jude to help. You haven't had any real help in almost a year, and we're starting to need it, badly. There's another one, as well—a kid. They both used to be with the Baldwin-Felts. He's been shot up some, but Warby is tending to him."

"Only a matter of time before he's back on his feet, then," said Lebo, flopping back on the sofa with a grunt. "So when can we pick up this new order?" he asked. Jude watched him closely, but he didn't bat an eye when Bishop mentioned the Baldwin-Felts, or Harvey being shot.

"I'll have a final word by the end of today," Bishop said. "Until then, you can make your usual rounds—and show Jude the ropes." Bishop glanced over at Jude. "He'll need a new set of clothes."

Lebo was picking at something between his back molars. "We've got extras," he said. "Don't pay no mind to any holes or stains you see on the shirts."

Bishop cast a dark look, and Lebo flung up his hands. "You got no sense of humor, Sid."

Lebo strode over to a narrow door in the wall and swung it open. Inside, Jude saw a set of bunkbeds lining the walls of a very small room, with more built-in cabinetry. Lebo pulled out a drawer, rifled through it, then pulled out a stack of clothes.

"I reckon these'll suit you," Lebo said, handing the stack to Jude. "You ain't putting them on before taking a bath, though. Lord Almighty, boy, you stink to high heaven."

Jude frowned, ducking his head to smell his shirtfront, and Lebo cackled, slapping him on the shoulder.

"Jude, Lebo will inform you about—" Bishop began.

"Get out of here, Sid!" Lebo said, making shooing motions with his arms. "You ain't doing us no good around here, not when that order needs filling."

Bishop headed toward the door, pulling out a watch from his pocket. "I'll send Monty with word," he said.

"Tell Monty to bring me some more chew," Lebo called as Bishop ascended back above deck. He chuckled to himself, then turned to Jude.

"Well, there ain't a bathtub on the Damsel," Lebo said, arms akimbo. "All I can offer you is a bar of soap and a bucket of water. But I tell you what, boy—I'll put on the kettle so it'll be hot water. Ain't that nice of me?" He grinned, showing all his missing teeth.

"Appreciate it," Jude said. He flopped onto the sofa, letting out a gust of air. The cabin was cramped and dark, but there was a comforting roughness about it. Jude watched as Lebo pulled out a dented copper kettle and settled it over a small stove in the corner, popping open the hatch beneath for a moment to stoke the coals. Warmth radiated throughout the tiny room, and Jude could hear Lebo singing "Shady Grove" under his breath as he latched the stove door shut again.

It occurred to Jude that he hadn't spent time in a real home for weeks—that is, if he could call his shabby rented room in Bluefield near the Baldwin-Felts office a home. He thought back on that room, remembering for the first time the engraving set he had left there. It was his first indulgent purchase over the nearly ten years he had been working for Baldwin-Felts: he had ordered a woodworking and engraving set from a catalogue and had even gotten some wood scraps from a nearby lumber mill to start on some more carving. Beyond that, he could think of no other valuable belongings left in that room. A badly-made bed, a small wardrobe, a cane-backed chair, and a noisy radiator— that was all that was left behind.

Stretched out on the sofa, Jude tried to conjure memories of that room. He thought of the other Baldwin agents hovering over a card game spread out over a patched bedspread—but no, that had been in someone else's quarters, not Jude's, and he had turned away the invitation to join. As for female companionship—he had learned early on that none of the local girls would pay mind to him or any of the other Baldwins. Rumors of Johnny Prince circulated among the brothel girls, and they wouldn't go near the agents, not for all the money in the world.

Jude rubbed his hands together, trying to stir warmth into his fingers. This was it, then—all he remembered of nearly a decade in that rented room. The nights he hadn't been drinking were spent in that room, sitting alone on the edge of his bed, staring at his hands, much as he was now. How could ten years go by with so few moments to think back on?

Jude squeezed his eyes shut, a subtle throbbing growing in his head. There were moments—moments he didn't want to remember. Threatening men in dark rooms, some of them unionizers, but some of them not. It hadn't mattered. The Baldwins were paid to hunt out the unionizers, like hounds flushing quail from a field, not caring if they crushed other creatures underfoot in their pursuit. Jude remembered evicting a family from their ramshackle hut in the middle of January, one of the other men—had it been Prince?—dragging the wife out by her hair when she struggled against them. The children, one as young as eight or nine, were smudged with soot from their shift in their mines that day. The husband had wept silently, collecting his family around him as snow fell on their shoulders. Where had they gone? Did they have any family that weren't also trapped in the mining villages?

Willis's face floated quietly into Jude's mind, smudged all over with dirt and coal dust. Jude had never looked at Willis's body once it was found, but he knew the way the methane gas would have made his brother's face grey, not white, the vacant eyes bloodshot from asphyxiation. There would have been gelled daubs of blood here and there, from where their father's belt buckle had gashed the skin. Willis had always taken the beatings without resisting, but that last time, he ran. He saw Jude watching, and he ran.

The kettle squealed on the stove, and Jude jumped. Clammy sweat glazed his chest and underarms, and he clutched his hands together to keep them from shaking.

Lebo lifted the kettle and poured the water into a tin bucket, clouds of steam billowing up into his browned face. "Here we go," Lebo said, lifting the bucket by its handle and taking it into the bunk room. Jude followed behind, his feet scuffing the floorboards, breathing deeply through his nostrils.

"Soap and towel are in there," Lebo said, rubbing his hands on his trousers. "Get on, now—and clean yourself proper. You reek something powerful."

"Yeah, I heard you the first time," Jude mumbled, closing the door behind him.

Jude dipped a rag into the hot water and dragged it across his skin, a shudder of relief passing through him at the warmth. After bathing, Jude pulled on the clean linen shirt Lebo had set out, his skin still flushed from the hot water. His wet hair fell into his eyes, but at least it no longer reeked of riverweed and sweat. There was a small mirror tacked onto the wall, and Jude examined what he could of his reflection. His face had tanned, and Jude thought he noticed elongated lines forming across his forehead. The dark eyes looking back at him were bloodshot.

Jude glanced away from the mirror and ran a hand over his clothes—they were plain but made of good cloth, warm and sturdy. Jude shoved the shirttails into his trousers and pushed back his hair. Looking back into the mirror, Jude acknowledged the beginnings of a beard covering his face.

"You got a razor?" Jude called through the door, lifting his head to look under his chin, where the hair was particularly thick and bristly.

"Sure do."

The door opened and Lebo came in with a razor folded in his hand. "Been a while since your last shave, boy. You're woolier than a sheepdog."

"Lost my set," Jude mumbled, taking the razor and testing it on his thumbnail—it left a fine, sharp line. Jude rubbed his face over again with hot water and began on the left side of his face. The razor made a clean swipe, and the bristles fell onto the top of Jude's feet.

"Haw, now, you're making a mess," Lebo said, scowling. "Didn't your daddy never teach you to put a bowl underneath?"

Jude shot Lebo an annoyed look through the mirror, but dragged the bucket of water over and set it below the mirror. He had learned to shave in the stable at the Wagners's house. Mrs. Wagner fussed at him to keep a neater toilet. At his first try, Jude had taken the razor to his dry face, resulting in a number of painful grazes. One of the other house hands had laughed at his scabbed face, and the next morning he found a shave brush and shaving bar on his cot. Eventually, he caught on how the process was done, but he got better at avoiding cuts once he took up wood whittling. Now, when he took the notion to shave, he found a certain pride in a close, clean shave.

"You'll want to trim up your hair, too," Lebo said. "You'll get words from Sid otherwise."

"So?" Jude asked, tucking his bottom lip under his teeth as he shaved his chin.

Lebo let out a huff. "Listen here, rooster. Sid got you a job, didn't he? And if he doesn't like his folks to look like hobos, then I'd be doing what I could to not look like a hobo, you hear?"

Jude met Lebo's eyes through the mirror. He was struck once again by Lebo's gaunt frame, but there was a steely brightness in his eyes.

"You're the boss."

Lebo's face eased up. "That's more like it," he said. "Hold on, I got a pair of scissors someplace around here."

Jude finished shaving and ran a hand over his face and neck. It felt good to be clean-shaven again. The itchiness was about to drive him crazy.

"Alright, Rapunzel," Lebo said, reentering the room. He grinned, holding up a pair of scissors.

The scissors were dull, and when Lebo was finished, Jude had a short and uneven fringe of hair. Jude ran his fingers back and forth through his hair, frowning slightly.

"Ain't you pretty now," Lebo said, wiping the scissors on his pant leg. "You hungry? I'll make you a bite to eat, then we can get going. Got a whole round to do today."

Jude's heart quickened as Lebo steered the Damselfly away from the docks. He could not remember ever being on a boat before in his life, and the gentle rocking motion was both disorienting and calming. He took a stale biscuit off the plate Lebo had left on the table and stuck it in his mouth, bounding up the stairs two at a time. A light breeze ruffled his shirt as he emerged above deck, and his still-damp hair felt cold on his scalp.

Lebo steered the Damselfly out into the center of the river. The current picked up around them. "We're heading to a couple little places on the river. They might have something for us, might not."

Jude sat down on the deck, stretching his legs out in front of him and taking a bite out of his biscuit. As they glided down the river, he watched as different birds waded in the reeds, or took sweeping dives toward the middle of the river. A gaggle of geese crowded near a sandy beach on the opposite side, making a racket. There were no other boats on the river.

"Here we go," Lebo muttered, steering the Damselfly up near a bank. Jude could see a split-log cabin camouflaged between some pines a few yards away from the river.

"Put these on," Lebo said, tossing Jude a pair of galoshes.

Jude tugged on the galoshes, finding them uncomfortably small. He and Lebo hopped over the side of the Damselfly, splashing into shallow, silty water. Lebo tied the boat to a half-rotted wooden post stuck into the clay, then waved an arm at Jude to follow him up the bank to the house. A narrow stream, barely just a trickle of water, ran past the little house, and on the stream was a metal still, poorly concealed by a few branches and bracken. The coils were down by the stream, cooling whatever distilled liquor passed through.

"Ms. Griggs lives here," Lebo explained in a hushed voice. "She ain't hardly got nothing to sell except a corn whiskey, and not much of it. But we check on her every so often to see if we can buy anything off her."

Lebo knocked on the door and stepped off the porch. A few seconds passed, and then the door slowly opened to reveal what Jude first mistook for a child, then realized was an extremely wizened old woman. She seemed to barely come up above the doorknob, and her wiry white hair was mostly undone from a loose bun on the top of her head. She peered out at them with bleary eyes that were half obscured by folds of loose skin and wrinkles.

"Ms. Griggs," Lebo said, nodding his head to the woman. "Came to see if you had any corn whiskey to sell us this week."

Ms. Griggs stared at them, her hand quivering on the doorknob. "What?" she whispered hoarsely.

"Corn whiskey," Lebo repeated, a little louder.

Ms. Griggs slowly shook her head. "No whiskey. Not today. I've—I've got…" She turned and disappeared into the cabin, leaving the door ajar. She returned with a little jar, which she seemed to struggle to carry.

"Mash," Ms. Griggs said, putting it into Lebo's hands. "Ain't gotten around to making it yet. I finished the—I finished the other one."

Lebo fished a few dollars from his pocket and laid them out in Ms. Grigg's gnarled hands, counting the amount out loud for her. Ms. Griggs stood still for a moment, staring at the bills lying flat on her palm. She then closed her fingers around the bills and hobbled back into the cabin, stopping to stare vacantly at them for a few moments before closing the door.

"She's up one hill and down the other," Jude said as they walked back to the boat.

Lebo sighed and shook his head. "Poor darlin' drinks half her own stuff. Don't have nothing to spend on food."

Jude gestured to the jar of corn mash in Lebo's hands. "What good's the corn mash to us? I thought you didn't have your own still?"

"We don't." Lebo waded into the river, hoisting himself up over the side of the Damselfly with a grunt. "I buy it from her, separate from Bishop's gig." He set the jar of mash on the deck, sighing again. "One day I'll knock on her door and ain't nobody will answer."

Jude looked at the little jar of mash. "Are all these stops going to be like this?"

Lebo made his way up to the pilothouse. "Naw. But that's a piece of it, mind you. These people up here are just trying to scrape by a living with whatever they have. Some are better at scraping than others."

They made four more stops along the river, one to a trade post with an enormous still in the cellar, two at fishing shacks on the river, the still coils dipping into the river like Mrs. Griggs's had. The inhabitants greeted Lebo gruffly, eyeing Jude with open distrust. Jude needed no interpretation when it came to the code of conduct toward outsiders. He helped load the liquor into the boat, but let Lebo do all the talking. The last stop was at another cabin just off the water, this one overflowing with children, who all ran out to meet Lebo. A few eyed Jude warily before proceeding to hop around Lebo, begging to be picked up.

"Haw, here we go!" Lebo called, lifting up a small boy and flinging him into the air before catching him again. The boy cackled wildly, screaming to be picked up again as soon as he was set down.

"Hey there, Lebo," greeted a man from the porch. "Come here to trade?"

"Yes sir, Mr. Tinsley," Lebo said. "Got a new partner with me today. This is Jude Washer."

"Come on out back," Mr. Tinsley said, casting an eye up and down Jude. "Littles—y'all stay here."

There rose a chorus of protests, and Lebo shot a glance at Jude over the children clustered around him. "I'll keep the young'uns occupied, Tinsley. Jude, you can handle this one." He handed Jude a roll of bills, giving him a look that Jude felt was supposed to convey a message. Mr. Tinsley frowned slightly as he led Jude to a back shed.

"If Lebo trusts you, guess that's about good enough for me," Mr. Tinsley said gruffly, fiddling with a lock on the shed. "Mind you, the littles don't know about all this."

He opened the shed door to reveal a sizeable still, and shelves loaded with bottles, some empty and clean, others already filled with moonshine. Mr. Tinsley began packing the bottles into burlap bags stuffed with straw, then handed the bags to Jude. Jude handed him the stack of bills. Mr. Tinsley's eyes fell away from Jude's face. They said nothing to each other as they walked back to the front of the yard, where Lebo was tossing more children around in the air.

"Well looky there, Mr. Jude's got some ni-ice bags of pelts from your pa!" Lebo shouted. "Got some squirrel? Any opossum?"

Jude hefted the sack on his shoulder and moved past them to the boat. Bishop had been a good liar—Lebo definitely was not. The children took no notice, just continued to cling to Lebo's arms and legs.

"Home again, home again," Lebo said, climbing over the side of the Damselfly. "Well, Jude, that's your first whiskey run over with. What'd you think?"

Jude shrugged, stretching himself back out on the deck. "I'll deal with old ladies and nutty kids over trigger-happy agents, any day."

The smile faded on Lebo's face, and he shook his head a little. "Well, I wish I could say it's only ever that. We do get some dirty players. The moonshiners used to go around shooting each other up until Jefferson and Bishop started buying their hooch and selling it to folks outside the cove. úCourse, that's about when Teague jumped in too and started buying. Turned out, that stirred up a lot of bloodletting too. It's how come we're so short-handed. Sounds to me like you ain't new to shooting, though."

Jude interlocked his fingers behind his head and closed his eyes, enjoying the pink warmth on his eyelids. Hillbillies shooting each other didn't seem so big a problem to him, laid out on the deck and smelling the faint algae odor of the river. The Baldwin-Felts and shooting and running were all miles and years away. All that was real now was the lapping of the Russet River on the side of the Damselfly, and the rows of mountain moonshine sloshing in their bottles.

Chapter Thirteen

"Lebo!" called a voice from outside. It was Monty.

Jude and Lebo were in the bunkroom below deck, dozing in the late afternoon. The bunkroom was small and chilly without the stove, but Jude was impossibly comfortable wrapped in a patchwork quilt. It smelled cottony and a little dusty, and the faint swirl of the water on the outside of the boat made it easy to drift into sleep.

Lebo propped up on one elbow in the opposite bunk, sniffing his nose loudly. "Come on down," Lebo yelled back, slinging his legs over the side of the bunk. Jude groaned as he felt the Damselfly tilt with the weight of someone stepping on board, and after a few seconds he followed Lebo into the other room. Monty reached the bottom of the stairs, and Harvey was behind him, his arm in a sling.

"Harvey," Jude said, stopping short.

"He insisted on coming where Washer was," Monty grunted, his hand discreetly gripping Harvey's arm. The boy looked like he was about to pass out again.

"Well sit down, before you don't have a choice," Lebo said, pushing a kitchen chair toward Harvey, who sat down heavily. A pair of woman's shoes appeared at the top of the stairs, and soon Warby was below deck with them.

"He shouldn't be moved in the first place," Warby said, brows drawn. "Lebo, he needs to lie down—"

"I'm fine, miss," Harvey murmured, leaning heavily on the table with his good arm.

"If you ain't a damn Clydesdale of a kid," Lebo said, looking Harvey over. "Glad to have you. Name's Lebo."

"Harvey Morgan," Harvey said, his head barely moving in an acknowledging nod.

"Hey Monty, did you bring me my snuff?" Lebo asked, slapping Monty's arm.

Monty grumbled and dug into his pocket, bringing out a little round tin. "No wonder you haven't got a tooth in your head," Monty grunted, and Lebo scowled.

"Lebo, I'm leaving this here with you," Warby said, holding out a small parcel. "Find someplace to put it where it won't fall down—they're supplies for Harvey's wound." Warby glanced up and her eyes met Jude's, her eyes roving quickly over his cut hair and clean face.

"I never looked at your arm," Warby said, slipping between Harvey and Monty to approach Jude. She was still wearing the bumpy old sweater over her dress, with her mousy brown hair tied back neatly. Up close, her face was remarkably young—she couldn't be much older than Harvey.

"Sid didn't say you was shot up," Lebo said.

"Just nicked," Jude said. "Don't bother with it," he said to Warby.

Warby's mouth sloped down slightly at the corners. "Well—it wouldn't be too bad an idea for you to keep cleaning it, too. Just ask Harvey—I've shown him how."

"Sure," Jude said, meeting Harvey's eyes above Warby's head. He was frowning.

"That'll warrant a thank you, I think," Monty said gruffly, arms crossed over his chest.

"Thank you," Jude said, glaring at Monty.

Warby reddened and stepped back to the stairs. "Well, if you're settled, then…" she began, looking at Harvey.

"Don't you worry úbout a thing, Miss Warby," Lebo spoke up, sounding boisterously loud after Warby's murmuring. "I'll get him set up with clothes and a bed and all the fixings. And we'll make sure he follows your orders," he said, lifting up the bundle of supplies.

"I appreciate it, Lebo," Warby said with a smile.

"I'll drive you home," Monty said, unfolding his arms.

"Miss Warby's a real peach, there," Lebo said, looking at the stairway after them. "Fixes us boys up after we've been roughed around. Seems like the squeamish kind, but she ain't." He clapped his big, hairy hands together abruptly, and Harvey jumped in his chair, followed by a wince. "Let's get you boys set up. It's nigh about dinnertime already, and I hit the hay pretty directly after. I've got some extra blankets in the bunker, and some shirts…" Lebo paused, looking Harvey up and down once more. "I declare, boy, you might just be too big for the shirts I got around here. If y'all can hang tight a minute, I'll run to the mercantile and pick you up some garbs."

"You don't have to bother with that," Harvey said.

"Shoot, Sid pays me back for just about anything I call 'company expenses.'" Lebo winked at them. "While I'm at it, I'll get us a bag of peanuts to shell, and some cola."

Lebo grabbed his jacket and bounded up the stairs, leaving Jude and Harvey below.

"Maybe you better lie down, Harv," Jude said. He grasped Harvey's good arm, and Harvey didn't protest as Jude helped him shuffle a few steps over to the sofa. A long silence stretched out, and Harvey's eyes glimmered bleakly across the room at Jude.

"You ain't sore with me, are you?" Jude asked. His hand went unconsciously back into his hair, unused to the shortness.

"Yeah, you could say I'm a little sore."

Jude exhaled heavily. "Look, I did the best I could with what I had," he said. "What else was I supposed to do?"

"I could have died from that meatball surgery you pulled on the train," Harvey said, sitting up halfway to glare at Jude. "She said it's a miracle I didn't bleed to death."

"You were bleeding anyway. The bullet had to come out, and I worked with what I had."

"About that," Harvey said, his voice rising. "Exactly how many bottles did you go through? From what I've heard we owe these people some sort of debt, which makes me wonder how the hell—"

"I didn't drink it all, okay?" Jude interrupted. "I'd be dead if I did, idiot."

Harvey scoffed and slouched back against the couch.

Jude ran a hand over his face, sighing. "I was pickled, I'll admit it. I probably used a whole bottle—hell, maybe two whole bottles—just on the damn silverware. And I gave some to you, and some to me, and—"

"That brings us to four bottles, just that."

"Well hell if I know," Jude exclaimed. He didn't want to rehash all this—it made him nauseous just remembering that night. "Some got smashed, or lost, or..."

"Look, forget about it. Neither of us were in great shape. But listen, you put these folks in a bind. Monty said—" Harvey leaned forward and lowered his voice to a raspy whisper—"Monty said this is a big bootlegging setup."

"Oh, is it?" Jude scoffed. "Look, where do you think I've been while you were being patched up? I struck a deal with them. Bishop wants us hired—running hooch and stuff."

Harvey let out a long sigh. "And you were stupid enough to agree?"

Jude leaned back against his chair, crossing his arms. "Look, kid, maybe you don't realize this yet, but we weren't going to make it just hitch-hiking down the mountains. This is a way to lay low and work for the time being."

"But—bootlegging?" Harvey looked Jude in the eye, and suddenly he was the farmboy saving pigs from the fire again. "You really want to get involved in something like that after all we just went through?"

"You see any other offers?"

Harvey closed his eyes, sinking deeper into the sofa. "I just thought we were done—"

"Done? With what?"

"Forget it," Harvey said, his eyes still closed. He looked weary and pale again, and Jude glanced at the sling cradling his arm.

"Look—don't worry too much about it," Jude said. "They

don't expect you to do anything for a while, not while you're like this. I'll do some work for them and get a feel for this crowd. If we don't like them, then we scram."

Harvey opened his eyes. After a moment, he nodded. "Okay, Jude," he said.

Chapter Fourteen

The gentle bobbing motions of the Damselfly woke Jude early the next day. The bunk room was almost completely dark, with the tiny porthole showing only a small glimpse of the purpling sky outside. Jude closed his eyes again, enjoying the slight rocking motion of the boat. After a couple moments, he sat up in bed and dropped lightly to the floor. Harvey was fast asleep in the lower bunk—breathing deeply, almost snoring—and Lebo was on the top bunk opposite, lying on his stomach so that he barely made any lump in the blankets at all. Jude quietly pulled on his jacket and snuck out the door.

Jude went over to the stairs and lifted the cabin hatch, emerging onto the upper deck. He inhaled sharply as the cold air hit him, driving all drowsiness out of his head. The sky was inky dark except to the east, where the horizon glowed like an amethyst. Jude rested his forearms against the railing, looking out on the river and rubbing his hands together to stir warmth. A fish jumped out of the water, leaving widening ripples on the surface, and a heron stirred in the reeds close to the boat. He stood there, listening to the sounds of nature, until the sun was halfway over the horizon and the sky had bloomed from purple to scarlet.

"Well, at least you've shown you ain't a bum."

Jude turned to see Lebo coming up the steps, holding two cups of coffee.

"Always my favorite time of the day," Lebo said, handing Jude one of the cups. "Ain't nobody else usually up by now."

Jude took a sip of coffee. It was bitter and still had coffee granules floating on the top, but it was warm and he enjoyed clutching the cup in his hands.

Lebo seemed completely alert, as if he had been up for hours. "This is a real special spot, right here. It ain't so bad living on the Russy."

Jude took another swig of coffee. None of the Baldwin-Felts had ever been this chatty first thing in the morning.

Lebo blew on his coffee to cool it, humming a few notes from a song. "Sometimes I could do nothing but this all day long. Just stare out on the river. But a man's got to make a living, don't he?" Lebo chuckled.

Jude grunted by way of conversation.

"Weren't making chicken scratch up where I used to be, way up in the hills. Had a fiancée, but her daddy made her break it off on account of me being so poor." Lebo stared at the heron in the reeds, and the shadows on his face made him look old. "Love's all heartache, Judy."

"Don't call me that."

"Right," Lebo said, and took a swig of coffee. He wiped his mouth with his sleeve. "How'd you and Harvey get so shot up?"

Jude cast a sideways look at Lebo.

"Haw, now, I told you my story," Lebo said, cracking a smile.

Jude shifted his weight, looking back out over the river. The heron stirred from the reeds and began to stalk out deeper into the river. "We were with the Baldwin-Felts breaking up a union," Jude began. "Things got hairy, one way or the other, and Harvey— we had to get him out of there."

"Well, as I'm hearing it, that about explains why Harvey's in hot water—but what got you all up in it?"

Jude looked down at his hands. "I wasn't thinking straight about it—just got him out of there. They would have killed him, otherwise."

"So if you was thinking straight, would you have left him there?"

Lebo was looking at him, but Jude turned his head. If Harvey had just kept his nerve during the raid, hadn't said those stupid things when Prince was near enough to hear—they'd be back in Bluefield instead of on the run. Thinking on that now, though, Jude wasn't so sure that was the alternative he wanted. What was waiting for him in Bluefield, anyway? A cold rented room, only ever leaving to head to coal mines to shoot at people and chase them out of their homes. And for what? Because the miners decided to go on strike? Looking out over the river, breathing clean air, it suddenly seemed outrageous to Jude.

A creak on the stairs made Lebo and Jude turn around.

Harvey was standing at the hatch. Though his face was cast in shadows, Jude knew he was looking right at him. He wondered how much Harvey had heard.

"There he is," Lebo said, breaking into his boisterous tone once more. "How about a cup of joe, Harvey?"

Lebo strode across the deck and descended down the stairs, hollering over his shoulder, "Y'all better get dressed. Monty'll be here soon."

Jude and Harvey met eyes as they stood at the top of the stairs. Harvey dropped his gaze and ducked back below deck.

Monty puttered up by the docks in the rickety automobile that had taken Jude and Harvey from the train station. Lebo wrapped a couple of stale ham biscuits in a towel and shoved it in his pocket, then motioned Jude toward the door.

"Harvey—you take care now," Lebo called over his shoulder. Harvey was stretched out on the couch, looking groggy. "Clean that hole out like Miss Warby showed you, hear?"

Jude put his hand on the passenger door when he came up to the car, but Monty gave him a dirty look through the window. He frowned and went into the backseat as Lebo clambered into the passenger side.

"Hey there, Monty," Lebo said. "Pretty morning, ain't it?"

Monty sighed, propping his elbow on the windowsill and leaning his head on his hand. "Do you always have to talk so much in the morning..."

They pulled away from the docks and the little town quickly disappeared from sight as they ascended into the woodlands. The ground was carpeted with thick fog that parted in soft curls as the car trundled along the road. Lebo began humming "Shady Grove" to himself again.

Monty drove till the land began to steepen and the road became more twisted. At one point Monty pulled up to a fork in the road and snatched up a slip of paper, holding it close to his face and squinting.

"What's it say?" Monty said, shoving the paper into Lebo's hand. "Can never read a word of Bishop's writing."

"Hell, I can't read," Lebo said. "Give it a try, Jude."

Jude took the paper, struggling to see the writing in the dim light. The words were written in a sweeping, spidery script. "Left at second bend," Jude read aloud. "Straight on road till trees clear."

Monty grunted and turned left. Before long, they saw the forest thinning, with lumber equipment visible through the trees. Then they came upon a clearing dotted with tree trunks, and a lumber mill up ahead. Monty steered them in front of the building and they climbed out.

"Ain't this...?" Lebo began.

"Yes," Monty interrupted. "Teague's territory."

Lebo whistled low under his breath. "Bishop must be in a real bind."

Jude recognized the name from earlier. "Who's Teague?"

"Leave the talking to me," Monty said, ignoring Jude as he glanced around the lumber yard. "This could get tricky."

The door to the lumber mill was propped open, so they walked through. A few men ambled about, sweeping sawdust off the floor and starting up the machinery. Monty approached one of the men and asked for a Mr. Anderson, and was pointed to a paunchy older man standing by a dusty looking desk.

"Mr. Anderson," Monty said, approaching the man.

"Morning," said Mr. Anderson, glancing up at them briefly before looking back down at a stack of papers he was rifling through. "What can I do for you boys?"

Monty cleared his throat, exchanging glances with Lebo and Jude. "We're here for the order called in last night."

Mr. Anderson opened a drawer and shuffled around inside before pulling out a carpenter's pencil. "Didn't get no orders last night."

Monty cleared his throat again, his thick mustache twitching. "'Twas a special order, Mr. Anderson," Monty said. "We're the Millers."

Mr. Anderson looked up sharply, his mouth falling open. "Millers?" he asked. "Now...wait just a moment, we don't..." Mr. Anderson turned and began shuffling the papers on his desk again. "No...afraid not. You boys are mistaken."

"Pop?"

A younger man strode forward, looking anxious. He cracked a smile and laughed. "Ah—you must be the Millers?" he said, extending a hand to Monty. "I'm...I'm Mr. Anderson. This is my father."

"What's going on here, Joshua?" Mr. Anderson demanded.

"Pops, they called last night wanting to place an order—" Joshua began in a low voice.

"We sell to Teague," Mr. Anderson hissed.

Joshua smiled nervously and pulled his father aside. They began to argue in hushed tones.

"Does this usually happen?" Jude asked, leaning against Mr. Anderson's desk. His eyes were drawn to a pile of wood scraps pushed into the corner. Pine, by the looks of it. Jude crouched and tucked a few pieces into his pocket.

Monty ran a hand over his face. "I've messed it all up," he grumbled.

"How'd Bishop manage to get in with Teague's folks?" Lebo asked, crossing his arms with a furrowed brow.

"Who the hell is Teague?" Jude asked again.

"Old rival," Lebo said. "Has a bunch of boys running through the hills, buying hooch off folks like we do. Gave us a lot of trouble at one time—a whole lot of trouble. He don't take kindly to competition. But Sid knows how to keep his head down."

"He used to," Monty grunted.

Joshua Anderson stepped away from his father, a strained smile on his face. "I sure am sorry about this," he said. "I've explained things to my father, and of course he understands now."

Jude glanced at Anderson Sr., who looked dark as a thundercloud.

"Please, follow me," Joshua said. He led them back outside toward a lichen-covered shed behind the lumber mill. Joshua fiddled with a padlock on the door and ushered them inside. He tugged at a cord hanging from the ceiling and a lightbulb clicked on, showing a row of short, bulbous brown bottles sitting on the floor.

"Apple brandy," Joshua said, pulling one off the floor. Monty took it from him, brushing a layer of fine dust off the sides of the bottle. He plucked out the cork and handed it to Lebo, who took a short sip.

"Sweeter than mother's milk," he said, grinning. Joshua smiled with relief.

"I've got two cases worth," he said. "And the price we agreed upon...?"

"It stands," Monty said, pulling out a wad of bills from his back pocket. He began pulling bills from the bundle and laying them into Joshua's hand.

Jude swore softly under his breath, whispering to Lebo, "You usually pay that much?"

"Sid always offers high for hooch, especially the good stuff," Lebo said from the corner of his mouth.

"Right," Jude said. "And how do I get the job of liquor-taster?"

Lebo gave a wheezing chuckle. "When you grow up on shitty hooch like I did, you learn the taste of wood alcohol real fast. Old Monty always gives me a taste before we buy from a new fella."

"Bring the auto round," Monty said, turning to Lebo. Joshua was pocketing the wad of bills and walking back to the lumber mill, looking flushed.

Lebo pulled the car back to the shed, and they began to load the bottles into the back of the car. It was a snug fit, and Monty took an old quilt and wound it in-between the bottles to keep them from knocking against each other.

"That'll about do it," Monty said, looking at the back of the car with some triumph.

Joshua suddenly came running toward them, waving his arms. "You have to leave," he whispered hoarsely when he neared them. "Teague just drove up."

"Damn," Monty said, closing the car hatch.

"We weren't expecting him," Joshua stammered. "He wasn't supposed to come for a week—"

"Come on," Lebo said. "Jude, get in the car."

"Do we have guns?" Jude asked, his heart beginning to pound.

"Yes," Monty said, striding toward the front of the car. "But I don't intend to use them till I have to." He opened the driver's door but didn't get in. "We can't start the car, they'll hear us. We'll have to push it a ways."

"Wouldn't it be easier to just scare them off with the guns?" Jude began.

"Dammit, Jude, just push!" Lebo snapped, opening his door and bracing his weight against the frame.

Jude rushed to the other side of the car, goosebumps climbing up his neck. All three of them began to push the car. It barely budged.

"Get back up there," Monty grunted to Joshua. "They'll start a shooting if they find us here."

Jude could hear his own heartbeat thundering in his head. He put his weight behind the push, and the car began to roll.

"Good, good," Monty panted. "We'll get it down to that dirt road."

They continued to roll the car across the dead grass and down to the red clay road. Once they were on the road, Monty ushered Lebo and Jude inside the car, glancing over this shoulder. Jude looked too, but could only see the back of the lumber mill and the hooch shed, the doors still wide open. Monty clambered into the driver's seat and started the car. Though they were a distance away from the lumber mill, Jude cringed at the sound of the engine starting.

"Go, go, go," Lebo muttered.

The engine flared to life and Monty eased into acceleration. Once they were a few yards down the road, he pushed down on the pedal and they zipped down the mountain.

"Hot damn," Jude breathed, resting his neck against the back of the seat and closing his eyes.

"Too close," Monty grunted.

"I sure hope those boys don't get busted up," Lebo said, sliding off his cap and sweeping a lock of sweaty hair off his forehead.

"What'll happen to them?" Jude asked.

"Nothing, God willing," Monty said, his mustache twitching. "But that depends if Teague buys their excuse."

"And if he doesn't?"

Lebo ran his hands up and down his thighs. "Won't be pretty. Teague ain't shy about using a gun. He killed off a bunch of our boys—killed Warby's daddy."

Jude sat up straighter. "Warby's dad? Bishop said he was a doctor."

"He was," Monty said. His voice always came out as a throaty growl, but there was a deep gruffness in it now.

"How'd he get wrapped up in a shooting?"

Monty ran a sleeve across his nose, staring rigidly ahead. "Teague led a raid on one of our bases, couple years back. Cowardly, rat-faced thing to do, if you ask me. Took a bunch of his men and they busted in on us. They'd been drinking, and we'd been drinking…"

"Back in the day, we'd drink as much of the haul as we wanted," Lebo interjected. "I don't recall why they was drinking so heavy that night, but half our boys couldn't even stand up straight when Teague busted in, bullets flying."

"It was a bloody massacre, that's what it was," Monty said. "Shot half of them dead where they stood. Moved upstairs where Dr. Jefferson was looking over inventory with Bishop. They heard the shots and Bishop pulled a pistol out, managed to pick some off—but not before they got to Jefferson."

Monty fell quiet, the jostle of the car the only noise for several seconds. "Jeffy was as fine a friend to me as anyone ever was," he started. "Losing her dad shook Warby up—shook us all up."

"Doc served us real well," Lebo said, patting Monty's shoulder with his hairy hand. "He was a mighty fine man."

"I'm alright," Monty said gruffly, shaking off Lebo's hand. "But Teague runs a dirty business, mark my words."

They bumped along the road for a few minutes, but drove past the road into town.

"Where are we going?" Jude asked, twisting in his seat to look back at the receding town.

"Oh, didn't we say?" Lebo said, turning to Jude with a grin. "We're going to the mill."

Chapter Fifteen

The car trundled down a hard-clay road running adjacent to the cloudy river. The woods became thicker until, all at once, they entered a clearing with an old stone mill perched alongside the river. Monty parked the car.

"What the hell is this?" Jude asked. He craned forward, peering at the wide, gray building through the windshield. The walls were made from hefty stones, each growing a fine stubble of lichen and moss.

"Welcome to the mill," Lebo said, throwing open his door. He climbed out and stretched his arms over his head.

It looked abandoned from the outside, and it was strangely hidden from the main road. Unless you were passing by boat along the river, you might never know the building was there.

"Let's hurry up and get inside, it's none too warm out here," Lebo said, thrusting his hands in his pockets.

"What about the hooch?" Jude asked, jerking a thumb toward their car.

"We'll get it, we'll get it," Lebo said, waving a hand. "Come on, I want you to see this place."

Lebo and Monty approached a door made of thick planks, the wood sun-bleached an ashen gray. Fine particles of dust swirled in the air as they entered the dark interior, a cavernous warehouse completely empty of any furniture. A row of narrow windows lined the high top of the walls, casting a weak light onto the dusty floor. It was a huge space, featureless but for an enormous grist stone near the center.

"What are you doing here?"

Jude, Monty, and Lebo turned to see Bishop emerging from a door on the other side of the room.

"Just showing Jude the place," Lebo said. "Won't be too long before he's in here helping."

"I take it the run this morning was successful, then?" Bishop said, approaching closer.

Monty and Lebo exchanged glances. "More or less," Monty said.

Bishop frowned and strode past them toward the door. "Meaning?"

"Meaning," Lebo said, hurrying to catch up with Bishop, "that Teague showed up and about busted our butts."

Bishop stopped, turning around. "Did he see you?"

"No," Monty said, crossing his arms over his chest. "Don't think so, anyway."

Jude leaned on the doorframe of the mill, listening to their conversation. He pulled out the chip of pine he had taken from Anderson's, fingering the grain of the wood. It was short and thick—perhaps he would make a spinning top out of it.

"Too risky for my liking," Bishop said. "Anderson will be in hot water, one way or the other. We need to check on him in a day or two."

"If there's anything to check on," Lebo muttered.

"Well, did he have the full order prepared? Apple brandy?" Bishop asked.

"Yep," Lebo said, pulling open the car door to show the cases of apple brandy.

"I'm not paying you to prop open the door, Washer. Come get this unloaded."

Jude looked up, stuffing the pine scrap back into his pocket. He strode over and helped Lebo lift the apple brandy out of the automobile. Bishop and Monty were standing to the side, murmuring about something.

Lebo led Jude across the cavernous main room into a smaller back room, which was stacked with a few bottles and casks.

"Hoo, this place is a mess," Lebo said, setting his crate on the ground with a grunt. A puff of dust rose up around his feet.

"What's the use of having such a big place?" Jude asked, pushing hair out of his eyes.

"Well," Lebo said, putting his hands on his hips and looking around, "it's out of the way, for one thing. We got it dirt cheap, too. But back in the day, we could really fill this place up. And we lodged here too—that was before we got the Damselfly."

"Lebo, Jude, come out here," Bishop called from the main room. "Listen, we've got a party order."

"What the hell's a party order?"

"We have a handful of clients from downstate who place large orders occasionally. They're usually planning some sort of large event," Bishop explained.

"How much do they want?" Monty asked.

"Enough for a hundred people, I'd say."

Lebo let out a low whistle. "We're going to have to do a hell of a lot more runs to get enough hooch for that, Sid."

Bishop nodded. "I know. And straight moonshine isn't going to charm this crowd. We'll have to collect as much variety as we can."

"Well, what else can y'all get around here?" Jude asked.

"Gin, whiskey, and fruit wines, mostly," Lebo said, ticking them off on his fingers. "What you reckon, Sid?"

Bishop ran a thumb over his bottom lip, thinking. "Whiskey's good. I can maybe get my hands on some bourbon from out of state—it'll cost a pretty penny, though."

"McGregor can get his hands on vermouth, time to time," Monty interjected. "We'd have to haul down to the midlands to meet him, but he's always looking for a trade."

"Good, good. Send a telegram tonight and see. I'll look into the bourbon. Lebo, Jude, double your runs. Head down toward Riggins and see if they have anything to offer there. Even if it's only moonshine, we need to have as much stock as possible." Bishop turned slightly, so that his back was to Lebo and Jude, but Jude could hear him murmur to Monty, "We need this, Monty. Make it happen."

The rest of the week, Lebo and Jude went out each day to a liquor vendor, most of them deep in the mountains. These vendors were different from the lumber mill they visited—they couldn't even drive up to half the shacks and crumbling log houses they stopped by. Many times, Lebo took the Damselfly down the river to reach an isolated cabin a few acres inland, or puttered directly up to a run-down dock house.

Harvey joined them when they took the Damselfly out. He was weaker from the blood loss than the wound itself, which was beginning to heal nicely, but some color had returned to his cheeks. Like Jude, Harvey did not seem to have any past experience with boats, and they both liked to lean against the railing, watching as fish swam murkily past the Damselfly. When they reached their next vendor, Jude told Harvey to stay on board.

"Take it easy, huh?" Jude said, following Lebo over the side of the boat. "Won't take but a second, and we'll be back."

The truth was, he didn't want Harvey to see the people selling them liquor. Jude had already imagined half of the self-righteous lecture Harvey would give him after seeing the sellers and the conditions they lived in. They were all more or less the same. A woman would emerge from one, offering two jugs of moonshine with a grim face, or an old man with arthritis-crippled hands would point them to a small cluster of gin bottles hidden under his porch. As soon as Lebo paid them, they all dropped their eyes and melted back into their dingy homes.

"This way of life is killing them," Lebo said once as they walked back toward the Damselfly after a run. "Plain as that."

"Nothing wrong with making a living how you can," Jude said. Pride was often the biggest obstacle to survival. You had to make money by whatever means you had available, and sometimes there weren't many options. Life here was not so different from the coal mines, the people wearing patchwork clothing and tucking rags into the broken holes of their windows. A little money from a hidden still would have gone a long way for people like the Myers family.

"It's not the poorness that bothers them," Lebo explained. "It's the moonshining."

"It brings in good money."

"Ain't enough to make things better though, is it? What you don't see is that these folks are neck-deep in the drink every bit as much as those pickled dandies we sell to." Lebo kicked a protruding root as they shuffled back to the boat. "They can't hold their head up doing work like this—scraping by a living úcause they don't have no other options. Against the law, too. These are proud folks, Jude."

"I grew up in a mine camp, Lebo. You don't get to talk to me about poor people." Jude hoisted up the cask of whiskey in his arms to get a better grip, tense with irritability. They were nearing the Damselfly. Jude could see Harvey stretched out on the deck, his arm still in a sling.

"Well then, you ain't so different from us after all," Lebo said. "But listen rooster, moonshining's a whole other game. It gets a grip on folks the way nothing else does. I've been in that spot, not too long ago. I was a drunk, making moonshine—some to drink, some to sell. I felt as low-down selling it as I did getting drunk from it. These ain't hicks back here, Jude. They're people, families. Kinsmen. They weren't made to slink around under rocks."

"Then why do you buy it from them?"

Lebo did not reply immediately. "I guess to keep them from killing each other. Once everybody got to making their own hooch, they ran out of people to sell to. Sid and Jefferson could get it out of the mountains, sell it to other folks. Didn't stop the shooting, exactly, but it helped." Lebo looked up, a wry smile on his lips. "I gotta believe something better's on the way, though. Sid's got a lot of ideas, you know. Just waiting for one to take root, that's all."

Their conversation cut short as they hauled onto the Damselfly. Harvey stood up and helped them load the bottles onto the deck with his good arm. Lebo cracked a joke which made Harvey laugh, but Jude ignored them and ducked below deck. The cabin was full of shadows, the portholes streaming in light so that they looked like perfect frames for the landscape outside: the river reeds, the red-clay bank, the rows and rows of trees. Jude dug a square of cornbread out of the pan on the stove, eating it distractedly before reaching for the knot of wood in his pocket to settle his restless mind. Jude glanced back out the porthole and started as he caught a glimpse of a man in-between the trees, but then the Damselfly bobbed with someone's movement above deck, and in the next moment the man was gone.

Jude could feel his heart beating quickly, too quickly for having seen what was surely an ordinary man—probably one of the moonshiners coming down to see the boat. The unbidden image of Johnny Prince came to mind, his head swiveling back and forth like a dog sniffing at the edge of a forest. He could not have seen them. He hadn't seen them. And if he had, there were two states between them now, and the many crossed lines of the Blue Ridge to follow down.

Harvey ducked below deck. "Everything alright, Jude?"

Jude glanced up at Harvey, then back out the porthole. "You seen anybody walking around while Lebo and I were gone?"

Harvey paused, stepping down into the cabin. His brow was

furrowed. "No, didn't see anybody. But I was asleep most of the time up there, if I'm honest."

"Dammit, Harvey, if you can't help with the hooch you could at least keep some sort of watch." There was still no sign of a man along the tree line—had Jude imagined it?

"What the hell's got you so riled?" Harvey asked, grabbing a poker and stoking the coals in the stove. "Bishop said they don't hardly get law enforcement up here."

"I ain't worried about bulls," Jude said. "But those Teague guys are still out and about, who knows if they've connected the dots about us and that lumber mill. And the Baldwins—"

"Baldwins?" Harvey's head snapped up. "You said we gave them the slip."

Jude grabbed another square of cornbread, taking a bite to give himself time to respond. He needed to reclaim his cool before he spoke again. "We did," he finally answered. "But I don't put much past Prince."

"How worried are you?" Harvey asked, facing Jude.

Jude nearly made a wisecrack—he didn't want Harvey worried, not when he was still patching up. But he couldn't shake the dread that had sunk into his stomach. He needed another pair of eyes.

"I'm just saying, keep your eyes peeled," Jude said. He clapped Harvey on the back, attempting an easy smile. "We got a pretty good thing going here, huh? Living on a boat, limitless access to hooch—we don't want anything messing that up, right Harv?"

Harvey looked less than reassured as Jude climbed the steps back to the deck. He felt cold.

❧

They docked near town, Monty's automobile idling on the road off the dock. Warby sat in the front seat, a medicine bag in her lap, and Bishop stood outside the car with his hands in his pockets. Jude and Harvey exchanged glances before following Lebo off the boat.

"Howdy, Miss Warby," Lebo said as they approached the car. "Y'all going someplace?"

"We all are," Monty grunted through the open window. "Hop in."

"Stay on the boat, Harv," Jude said as he crawled into the back seat.

"I'm coming," Harvey said, ducking in after Jude.

"As you like it," Bishop said before Jude could protest. Warby slid over to make room for Bishop in the front seat.

It was a tight fit with all six of them squeezed into the automobile. Jude glanced behind their seat to see if there was any extra room, but instead found a couple rifles and some pistols scattered over the floorboard. He turned around to face the front, frowning.

"Bishop, where the hell—?" he started to ask.

"Bishop wants to check on those Anderson lads," Monty said.

"I didn't like the sound of it, the way it went down," Bishop said, watching the scenery out the window. "We owe them an apology."

"For what?" Harvey asked. His back was pressed against the door of the car to avoid crushing his shoulder, his neck craned over.

"Seems like Teague is the one who should apologize," Jude scoffed. "What did we do besides give Anderson a heap of money for his hooch?"

"I bartered a deal with him when I knew he sold to Teague," Bishop said. "Teague's kept his distance but only because we haven't encroached on his territory."

"It was still Anderson's decision to sell to us," Jude pointed out.

Warby said nothing, watching the road roll out in front of them, the sunshine glinting on her spectacles.

"Jude's right, Sid, you got no reason to worry," Lebo said.

"I'm not worried," Bishop said.

Jude glanced behind them again. "Sure you're not. Must be why there's all these firearms back here."

Lebo and Harvey twisted in their seats to peek behind them, then met each other's eyes. Jude could see Warby's hands tighten on the medicine bag.

They drove up to the lumber yard. Even though it was midday, there were no men walking around. Jude elbowed Harvey until he opened the car door and they tumbled out. Jude reached behind him and tucked a pistol into his belt when Harvey had his head turned. Something was off.

Monty must have sensed it too, because he opened his door and muttered, "Come on," to them, striding toward the mill. Harvey closed the automobile door slowly, tense as a buck walking into an open field. The eerie silence reminded Jude of the miner's camp when the Baldwin-Felts had begun their raid; he wondered if Harvey was thinking of that, too. He was beginning to wish he had grabbed a gun for Harvey, too—just in case. Jude could hear a saw running idle in the back of the mill, but there was no sound of cutting or lifting wood.

"Hello?" Jude called out. Lebo and Monty turned to him, surprised to hear him call out first. Warby and Bishop approached behind, their eyes roaming over the scene. Jude walked into the shade of the mill, uneasiness making his hands twitchy.

"Who's there?" came a quavering voice.

Jude thought Monty would answer, but Monty nudged Lebo, who spoke up. "Hey there, it's Lebo. Where's everyone at?"

"Get—get out of here," the voice stammered. A shape materialized out of the shadows, and Joshua Anderson approached them warily, a shotgun in hand. Monty, Lebo, and Bishop all lifted their hands; Harvey reached his good hand over and rested it over his sling, his eyes alert and unblinking. Warby held her bag in front of her, Bishop moving her behind him. Jude did not raise his hands.

"Easy now," Jude called out, his heart hammering. It took all his self-control not to whip out the pistol in his waistband.

"Shut up," Monty said out of the corner of his mouth. "Let Lebo handle this."

"What's all this for?" Lebo said. He kept his voice at a drawl, without any hint of a quaver or tension. He seemed unruffled looking down the barrel of a shotgun.

"I was a fool to sell to you," Joshua said hoarsely, the shotgun quivering in his hands. "Teague found out, and he came back."

"Where is everyone?" Bishop asked.

"Gone," Joshua said. A cloud lifted and shone a thin ray of light into the mill, and Jude saw with a turn of his stomach a blue and purple bruise running from Joshua's temple down to his jawbone—the shape and size of a rifle butt. Warby inhaled sharply and made a move forward, but Bishop dropped his arm down to block her.

"Teague and his boys came and shot daddy, and half killed the rest of us. None of my men will come back to work. Daddy, he's—" Joshua swallowed visibly. "He ain't likely to come through."

"Son of a bitch," Lebo said. His mouth was turned into a deep frown, the creases in his face making him look older than usual.

"Please," Warby said, pushing past Bishop, her eyebrows drawn together. "Let me take a look at your wounds. I could help your father, too."

"Get back," Joshua barked, swiveling his gun to Warby.

"Hey!" Jude whipped the pistol from his belt. Bishop and Monty surged a half-step forward, then froze.

"Cool it, Jude," Lebo snapped. "Put it away. Warby—" He reached out, and Warby shuffled over to him, her face white as she glanced between Joshua and Jude.

"I don't ever want to see y'all again," Joshua said, gripping the shotgun tighter. Jude shifted, moving his body halfway to block Harvey. Joshua glanced at him sharply, continuing, "I should have never messed with our deal with Teague."

"Teague's business is in fear," Bishop spoke up. "You're in for more of this with him, whether you sell to us or not."

Joshua cocked the shotgun. "Get out!" he yelled.

"Come on," Lebo mumbled, laying a hand on Warby's shoulder as they backed slowly toward the car. "We can't help here."

Jude lowered the pistol as he opened the back door and pushed Harvey forward. "Get in, get in," he muttered.

At that moment, Jude caught the sound of tires rolling over gravel. He looked behind them to see another car trundling up the road. He couldn't see who was inside the car, but the hairs stood up on the back of his neck.

"Harvey—take one of those guns," he whispered.

"Huh?" Harvey glanced behind them to where Jude was staring. Monty and Bishop had noticed, too. Jude reached into the back and pulled out the first gun he reached, thrusting it against Harvey's chest.

"Teague," Bishop said, gripping Warby's arm.

A look of sickened terror passed over Joshua's face. "Y'all get out of here," he rasped. "Get out!"

The car was already parked and five men climbed out. They were all gripping rifles. The car rocked beside Jude as Harvey emerged, coming alongside Jude with the gun held discreetly by his leg.

"Harvey get back in—"

"If you tell me to get out of the way one more time, I'll shoot you myself," Harvey murmured.

"Quiet, both of you" Bishop snapped.

"Mr. Sidney Bishop," the man shouted, stopping a few feet in front of the car. He had a hoarse, smoky voice, and his face was creased like old leather. "You know, I could have put money on you coming out this way today. You got a habit of paying calls after a purchase, you know that?"

"Let's work this out, Teague," Bishop called out, spreading out his palms.

Teague shook his head. "Now why should I trust a businessman who don't conduct fair business? Anderson's been selling to me for years, what made you think you could hop in?"

"Your quarrel is with us, Teague, not with Anderson," Monty spoke up.

"Or his men," Warby said, stepping out from behind Bishop. Her spectacles had slid halfway down her nose, her brows drawn tight together. "What business did you have in shooting those mill workers? Their business is in lumber, and that's all."

"Warby," Bishop whispered. He was white as a sheet.

Teague lifted his chin, gazing down the bridge of his nose. "Is that Warby Jefferson I hear? Well I'll be damned. Bishop, you're none too smart to bring your dame out on a run."

Warby colored, gripping her medical bag tighter. "Mr. Teague, you and your men better move on. You've done too much damage already—to folks that don't deserve it."

"That's not how I see it, miss," Teague said. The men behind him were ambling forward.

"Shit," Jude muttered. "Oh, shit, shit, shit." He could hear Harvey starting to breathe heavy beside him. He glanced at the boy and saw sweat slick on his brow. Jude's own heart was already hammering.

"Let us settle the score, Teague," Bishop spoke up again. "Name your price."

"I ain't worried about money, Bishop," Teague answered. "It's territory I'm worried about—and you've crossed a line." With a jerk of his arm, the barrel of Teague's rifle hopped up and landed in his hand.

"Warby—!" Bishop lurched forward and yanked her down just as a boom from Teague's rifle rang out. There was a metallic pop as the bullet hit the top of the automobile and ricocheted off.

Jude yelled and shoved Harvey back into the car. Two more shots rang out, and Jude frantically grabbed at the guns in the back seat.

"Jude—" Harvey looked like he was about to be sick.

"Get in the mill, Harvey, get high up. I'll cover you," Jude said, his arms full of guns. Teague's men were surging forward toward the car. "Go, now!"

Jude stumbled out of the car and rapid-fired behind him at

Teague's men as Harvey lurched forward and loped toward the mill. Jude ducked behind one of the opened car doors, taking a second to glance behind him. The others must have retreated back into the mill. Jude could only hold one pistol, his other arm wrapped around the other rifles he had grabbed. He could hear Teague's men shouting and starting to spread out.

Idiot, idiot, idiot. He had to be the one to grab the guns instead of retreating into the mill. Jude puffed in and out, in and out, preparing to run for it. He hopped up and fired another few rounds, then sprinted as fast as he could toward the mill. More shouts, more bullets—one audibly racing right past his ear. Jude was staggering now, his legs going too fast for him to keep balance. He dove into the mill just as the doorway was peppered with bullets.

"Are you shot?" Monty asked, gruffly lifting Jude to his feet as Bishop slammed the door shut.

"No—here—take these," Jude panted, pushing the guns into their arms. "Where the hell's Harvey?"

"Somewhere in here," Bishop said, backing away from the door and grabbing one of the guns Monty handed him. "Lebo went with Warby wherever Anderson ran off to. Come on, they'll be making for the other entrances. Washer—can you take care of yourself?"

They all jumped as Teague's men rattled the door, snarling curses before their voices faded away. They were spreading out. Jude heard shuffling footsteps from the upper loft in the mill.

"Don't worry about me," Jude answered, jogging toward the staircase to the side. "Harvey?"

"Here," he heard the boy whisper hoarsely.

Jude joined him in the loft, finding Harvey pressed against a wall near a window frame, turning his head cautiously to peer outside. Jude crouched down and joined him by the window.

"Two coming round back," Harvey whispered. "Can't see the others yet."

"We can pick them off before they get to that back door," Jude muttered, feeding more bullets into his pistol.

"Dammit Jude, you gave me a rifle," Harvey said. They both flinched as they heard a couple shots boom out from below in the house. Teague's men scurried into the bushes, hollering at each other—Monty or Bishop must have fired a warning shot.

Jude peeked around the window once more. "So? Come on, they'll start closing back in any second now."

"I can't hold it," Harvey snapped. He held the rifle in his free hand, the other arm still hugged close to his body by the sling. "It'd be nice if I had two loose hands, but I don't, in case you forgot."

Jude grunted. "Here, switch with me."

Jude took the rifle, handing Harvey his loaded pistol. He checked the rifle's cartridge before peeking around the window, only to duck back down again as the window panes splintered with a bullet, showering glass over them. Harvey stumbled back with a yell, a stream of blood trickling down his forehead where a small shard of glass had stuck. Jude's heart roared like an engine, and he spluttered out a stream of curses as he felt bits of glass imbedded into his ear and hair.

"Harv—hold on," Jude yelled. He glanced back out the window. One of the men crouched behind a tree. Jude didn't have a clean shot, but he could probably nick him. He raised the rifle into the shattered opening, resting it on the window frame—his hands were shaking too hard to hold the gun steady. He shot, seeing the bark on the tree chip off near the man's shoulder. The man hollered, dropping to his stomach before immediately getting up and running. Jude followed him with the barrel of his rifle, took his second shot—the man screamed and fell to the ground, clutching his side.

"Son of a bitch," Jude grunted, withdrawing the rifle and brushing at his hair to shake out the glass. His hand came back with fine streaks of blood, but it wasn't much. He turned back to Harvey. "Hey, hey, quit that," he barked, catching Harvey trying to pull out the bit of glass.

"God, it hurts," Harvey panted, blinking rapidly to keep the blood out of his eyes.

They heard more shooting outside, one of Teague's men yelling about the man Jude had shot. They would really start pressing in now.

"Alright, come on—Warby's in here somewhere with that medical bag, she can get you cleaned up." Jude took hold of Harvey's good arm, feeling a slight tremor in the boy's muscles as he steered him back toward the stairs. There was more shooting and yelling—Jude just hoped it wasn't from the Millers.

Jude kept his rifle up, coming slowly down the stairs and scanning the room below. It was empty. Through a doorway he could see a sort of warehouse, where piles of lumber were stacked. He could just make out the shape of Monty beside a door, his pistol poised in the air. He turned sharply as he saw Harvey and Jude enter, then immediately returned his gaze outside the doorway. Lebo and Warby were toward the back, where there were no windows. Lebo leapt up when he saw them.

"God Almighty, is he shot?" Lebo asked. Warby was crouched beside Joshua Anderson, who laid propped beside the wall, his eyes pinched shut in pain. She glanced up at Lebo's words, her mouth falling open before turning to pull bandages out of her bag.

"No, glass cut," Jude said. "Where's Bishop?"

"Quiet," came Bishop's hiss. He stood by a window, pressed against a wall. "Teague and two others—coming this way."

Jude left Harvey in Warby's hands, rushing over to Bishop's window as Lebo ran to join Monty on the other side. Jude glanced out the window—one of the men was half support-ing, half dragging his wounded comrade, the one Jude had shot, back toward the car. The fourth man was walking inde-pendently but bleeding heavily from his arm. The fifth man was not around—Bishop or one of the others must have shot him. Teague was clearly visible crouched behind a wheelbarrow in the yard.

"It's a clear shot, Sid," Jude whispered. "Take it."

Bishop stared out the window, his rifle poised but not aimed. Jude glanced between Teague and Bishop. "Sid," he hissed. "Take the damn shot." Nothing. "If you don't get him now, he'll come back later with twice the number of men."

"So I should kill the rest of them now, is that your advice?" Bishop's eyes were still fixed on Teague behind the wheelbarrow.

"You either take care of them now, or they take care of us later," Jude said.

"They're moving on," Bishop murmured. It was true—the other four men were already slinking back toward their car. "They know they're outnumbered." He withdrew his rifle from the window.

A shot rang out, and Teague screamed in pain. Jude whirled around to see Harvey crouched at the other window, a smoking pistol in his hand. Teague clutched his shoulder, where dark blood bubbled through his fingers.

"Harv," Jude said, a chill raining down his spine. There was a large bandage affixed over his left brow, but in his eyes was a chilling detachment that Jude recognized. It was the same remote coldness he looked for his flask to give him before raids.

Bishop swore loudly. Teague stumbled back toward the car, and with a skittering of gravel they disappeared down the road.

"What the hell was that?" Bishop yelled, rounding on Harvey.

"He was in plain sight, I took the shot," Harvey said, his face flushing. Jude could see the vacancy fading from his eyes as the old apprehension returned.

"They were already in retreat," Bishop shouted, flinging his arm out. "What made you decide to just—"

Jude batted Bishop's hand away. "Hey, lay off the kid, alright?"

Harvey was yelling now, his face dark red. "He shot all those other men, he came back to kill us too. What did you think we were—"

"They were in retreat," Bishop repeated, his own face darkening as he pulled up close to Harvey.

"You don't trust me or something?" Bandaged up as he was, Harvey still loomed an impressive figure over Bishop. "You think I'm not good enough to make that call, is that what this is? You wanted to pick him off yourself?"

"Harv, knock it off," Jude said. Blood was starting to seep through Harvey's bandage. Warby had her head turned, staring angrily at the wall.

"Both of y'all, shut up and back down," Lebo barked, coming between them. "Good God, y'all both cutting fools out of yourselves."

Monty stood close to Bishop, a hand on his shoulder. Jude heard him murmur into Bishop's ear: "The boy was only trying to protect the lot of us."

Bishop shrugged off Monty's hand, the veins in his forehead still prominent. "We need to clear out of here. We'll have to take Anderson someplace else, we can't leave him here. They may come back."

"I know his place, I can drop him off there," Lebo said.

"Fine." Bishop wiped his face with a handkerchief before lifting his eyes back to Harvey. Harvey stood his ground, but the flush was gone from his face.

"You did what you thought was best," Bishop said stiffly to Harvey. He turned toward the others. "In the car. Everyone."

Lebo took one of Anderson's wagons to take him to his home. The others clambered into the car, Jude pushing the rifles and pistols into the back. Warby was crying quietly in the front seat. Harvey's face remained a steel mask, but Jude caught sight of his one free hand shaking before he shoved it into his coat pocket.

Chapter Sixteen

Jude was shaken awake the next day, finding Bishop standing over his bunk.

"What the hell?" he mumbled.

"Don't wake the others," Bishop said in a low voice. "Come up on deck."

Jude grunted, tugging on a pair of trousers over his longjohns. He shambled after Bishop, grabbing a cup of cold coffee on the table that someone had left out the night before.

"What's so important that you had to get me up here on my own?" Jude asked, squinting against the flicker of sunshine glinting over the water.

"I know we all had a rough time yesterday, but I need your help with something," Bishop said. How he could look so clean and polished at the crack of dawn was beyond understanding.

"Well do you mind explaining quickly so I can get back to bed?" Jude took a sip of coffee and grimaced—ice cold.

"What happened yesterday," Bishop began. "Harvey—has he done much shooting before?"

Jude's morning grogginess dissipated with a flare of agitation. He crossed his arms over his chest. "Since you're asking, no. He hasn't."

Bishop nodded slowly. "That shot he made—"

"Yeah," Jude interrupted. Not only had Harvey's decision to shoot been unexpected, but the actual shot had surprised Jude—the aim was better than he had expected from the boy. "Surprised me just as much as it did y'all. But listen, he's not a rough kid, he's—"

"He didn't have to take that shot, though," Bishop cut in. "They were in retreat."

Jude thought they had left all this behind at the lumber mill. "What's your point?"

Bishop didn't reply immediately. He tapped his foot on the deck, once, twice, three times, as though measuring his next words. "I took a risk bringing you two aboard," he said at last. "Considering the way we found you, and what I know about you…I've questioned my decision more than a few times."

Anxiety simmered in Jude's stomach. He shifted his weight from one foot to the other. "This sure was worth getting out of bed for, let me tell you."

Bishop held up his hand. "Let me get to my point."

"I wish you would." Jude took another sip of coffee, more to do something with his hands than because he wanted more of the drink. He tried to imagine it piping hot.

Bishop glared at him. "I've observed something from both of

you that I believe puts my questions to rest, regardless of my other apprehensions."

"And that would be…?"

"Loyalty," Bishop said.

Jude snorted. He thought of Bradshaw's face when Jude shot him in the leg.

"Yes, I mean it," Bishop said. "To each other, and to the peculiar set of values you keep. And if I can tap into those values, I believe I can earn your loyalty, too."

Jude rolled the tin coffee cup idly in his hands, careful not to betray his piqued curiosity. "What values?"

Bishop crossed his arms, looking down his nose at Jude with an appraising eye. "The same values we keep around here. Independence. Dignity. Brotherhood. The importance of those things in combination."

Jude ran his thumb over the lip of the cup, nodding slowly. "Maybe. Maybe not."

A slight smile flickered on Bishop's face. "I'll let you keep your cards close for now. But I've got enough faith in my hand that I'm willing to gamble. I believe I have a plan that you'll want in on."

"What kind of plan?"

Bishop turned to look out over the river, watching as a heron glided over the surface with ghostlike grace. He exhaled slowly, his breath coming out in a cold cloud. He looked tired, all of a sudden. "A plan to get us out of this hell we call bootlegging."

"Lebo says it's the only way to make money up here."

"I hope to prove him wrong," Bishop said. "But before the end, we'll need as much hooch as we can get for this order. The money's the only thing that will make this work."

"You going to clue me in on anything else, or am I supposed to just listen to you talk in riddles forever?"

Bishop let out a low laugh and turned to look at Jude, this time with shrewdness in his eyes. "Just because I'm ready to take the gamble doesn't mean I'm showing my hand yet. But suffice it to say this: if we can pull off this order, I have a plan in place that will free us from the hooch business. No more guns, and no more shooting from Harvey."

Jude's gaze snapped up to meet Bishop's.

"I saw your face," Bishop said. "Don't think that I don't know what it feels like, to see the people you care about slowly corroded over time."

They ran orders nonstop for the next two weeks. It was constant work, and more challenging—they were constantly on edge looking for an ambush from Teague. The Millers started taking the back roads of back roads—narrow paths Lebo called "deer trails"—and only ran orders on the river in the hours just before dawn and after dusk. The liquor room at the mill became fuller and fuller, until eventually they had to spill over into another storeroom.

After docking the Damselfly late one night, Lebo, Monty, Jude, and Harvey sat slumped at the kitchen table.

"One hell of a day," Lebo said. "A bit of grub would do me a world of good."

"I could use something stiffer," Jude said.

"Not a bad idea."

Monty stood with a grunt, reaching into one of the lower cabinets and pulling out a bottle by its neck.

Jude flicked a thumb at the cabinet. "You never told me that was in there."

Lebo chuckled. "If I had, it wouldn't be there now, would it?"

Harvey snorted a laugh, and Monty tugged the cork out of the bottle, sloshing some of its contents into four tin mugs.

"To running hooch," Monty said, sarcasm heavy in his voice as he raised his mug.

"To hooch," Jude said, tossing back the drink. It burned hot in his throat, bringing tears to his eyes. He sucked in a hoarse breath, drawing barks of laughter from Monty and Lebo. They downed their drinks in a gulp, letting out a growl after swallowing, and laughed again. Harvey held his mug in his hand, staring into it without saying anything.

"Food!" Lebo said, snapping his fingers. "I'll rustle something up before we get too dog-gone drunk."

"Put on some bacon, Lebo," Monty said over his shoulder. "Patsy's fed me nothing but salt cod for nigh a week now."

"Coming right up."

The Damselfly tilted suddenly, and all four of them fell silent.

"Someone's aboard," Monty murmured, shoving the bottle under the table.

Footfalls came from above, and a pair of polished leather shoes appeared on the steep stairs.

"Haw, it's just Sid," Lebo said, turning back toward the stove.

"I expected you all at the mill a good hour ago," Bishop said, ducking as he joined them below deck.

"We've been and gone by the mill, already unloaded the stock," Monty said, pulling the bottle back up to the table.

"Enjoying some of the wares, are we?" Bishop and Harvey exchanged wary glances—both had been standoffish of each other since the shooting at the lumber mill.

"You'd join us if you been working as hard as we have," Jude said, dragging a fifth mug across the table and sloshing some liquor in.

"Feels like we've been all over the county, and then some," Harvey broke in. "Seems like there ain't nobody who don't have moonshine to sell. Everybody's making it." He tipped the contents of his mug into his mouth, wincing as he swallowed. The four others watched him, Lebo letting out a low whistle.

"Easy there, Harv," Jude said, cracking a grin. He grabbed the bottle to pour more into Harvey's cup. "Just when exactly did you learn to take your liquor?"

"Picked it up on some train," Harvey mumbled.

There was silence but for the sizzling bacon for several seconds, then Jude felt something like a bubble rise in his chest, and all at once he erupted into laughter. Harvey smirked into his cup and took another swig, and Bishop leaned back in his chair, a chuckle rolling out from his throat. More liquor went into each of their cups and Monty brought out a deck of cards.

"Deal me in," Lebo said, flipping the bacon. "Lord Almighty, if heaven don't smell like bacon, just send me straight to hell."

"Want me to hold your cards, Harv?" Jude asked, leaning toward Harvey's chair.

"Buzz off," Harvey said, shoving Jude away with his good arm.

"I should take this bottle out of your pay," Bishop said, shaking the bottle above their heads so they could hear the empty space. He had shrugged off his jacket and loosened his tie, the most laid-back Jude had ever seen him.

"You'll have to take it out of your own, too," Monty said, lifting up Bishop's mug and swaying it so they could hear the slosh of liquid inside. Bishop snatched the mug out of his hands with a laugh, tossing back the rest of the liquor.

"God," Bishop sighed, banging the mug back down on the table. "There's got to be a better way to make money up here."

Jude glanced sideways at Bishop. He hadn't forgotten their early morning discussion from a couple weeks ago.

"You could go into the lumber business, Sid," Lebo said, tossing one card into the middle of the table before walking back to the stove. "Who wants cornbread?"

Harvey raised his hand before throwing one of his cards onto the table. "Lumber's about as dangerous as bootlegging," he said. He snuck a sideways glance at Bishop.

"Boy's not wrong," Monty said. "I've heard they lose a man nigh every day in some camps. I'll take some cornbread, Lebo."

"My question is, if you want to make money, what the hell's keeping you here?" Jude asked, fingering his cards. Lebo started chuckling by the stove.

"What?" Jude said, twisting in his seat.

"Well go ahead, Sid," Lebo said. "What the hell's keeping you here?"

"That's personal," Bishop answered, the stony demeanor dropping over his face once more. Monty grunted, staring at his cards.

"Let's just say," Lebo began, tipping cornmeal into a rough wooden bowl, "it ain't so much him who wants to stay here."

Bishop laid his cards face-down on the table, glaring at Lebo. Lebo grinned back at him.

"Y'all talking about Warby?" Harvey asked, reorganizing the order of his cards.

Bishop's head whipped around to Harvey, who started laughing.

"Look, you'd have to be blind to not—"

Lebo let out a whoop by the stove, his eyes pinched shut in laughter. "Sid—so much for—so much for 'mask of discretion,' huh?" He dissolved into wheezing cackles.

Bishop pulled Lebo's mug out of reach. "You shouldn't be drinking while you cook."

"Come off it, Bishop," Jude said, drawing a card. "It's clear as crystal y'all are a pair."

"If you need to know, Warby considers this her home, and so I must make ends meet here. Are you satisfied?" Bishop picked his cards back up with a flick of his wrist. "Your turn, Lebo."

"Put down that third card to the left, Jude," Lebo said, cracking an egg into the bowl. "What is it?"

Jude flipped over the card. "Three of spades."

"Damn. Should have said third to the right."

"Warby never said anything about being engaged," Harvey said.

"Why should she?" Bishop asked, thumbing through his cards. "It doesn't concern you."

Jude smiled into his cards. "I think Harv caught some Florence Nightingale syndrome for our Warby."

"Shut up, Jude."

"Now, now," Lebo said, turning back toward the table and stirring the cornbread batter, "we've all had a sweet spot for Warby at one time or another. She's a real dime."

Jude thought about Warby, with her rectangle spectacles and dumpy sweaters. He found it hard to imagine the appeal, but he wasn't about to say that in the present company.

"I got into the business years ago with Warby's dad," Bishop said, laying down a card, "and somehow took on his work after he was killed." Bishop frowned, picking up his mug for another swig of liquor. "I promised him I'd provide for Warby, and I won't break that promise. But this damn hooch business..."

"Speaking of which," Monty interrupted, looking at them

over his cards. "I caught a whiff of Prohibition agents in town today."

Jude and Harvey sat up straight in their chairs, exchanging glances. "What do you mean?" Jude asked.

"They come sniffing around from time to time," Bishop explained. "But it's been a while since they've come this far into the mountains. You sure they weren't just some cops looking into Teague's men?"

"I didn't see them myself," Monty said, "but Patsy said a couple bulls were lurking at the post office asking questions. She felt pretty sure."

"Better lay low till they pass on," Bishop said. "Lebo, take extra precautions on your last rounds tomorrow. Let's keep on the river, they usually don't bother us out there. They've never found the mill before now, but we'll have to keep extra watch, just in case."

"Rest easy, boys," Lebo said, catching sight of Jude and Harvey's stiff postures. "Ain't nothing we haven't dealt with before."

Jude reached for the bottle to pour himself another drink, thinking of the man he had seen in the woods.

Chapter Seventeen

Harvey's arm was finally out of the sling, though Warby had made him swear to not lift anything with that arm for another few weeks. He was already violating his oath, however—Jude caught him grabbing a cask of liquor from the boat and carrying it into the mill.

"Harv," Jude called after him.

Harvey waved him off, casting a grin over his shoulder. Jude could tell he was feeling like himself again. He shook his head, hopping aboard the Damselfly to hoist up two clay jugs with a grunt. Lebo followed close behind, whistling a tune as they unloaded.

Jude and Lebo climbed the short hill up to the mill, entering into the dim interior. It was nearly dusk, and Bishop had laid a few lanterns on the floor. He had a clipboard in his hand, which he was struggling to read in the poor light.

"How much left, Lebo?" Bishop asked.

"Just two more casks and we'll be about done, near as I can tell," Lebo said.

Jude entered the storeroom behind Harvey, resting the jugs down on top of a crate. The storeroom was stacked high now, leaving very little floor space. Harvey rolled his shoulder experimentally with a slight scowl after setting down his cask.

"You really don't know how to follow orders, do you?" Jude asked.

Harvey let out a dry laugh. "I ain't worried about it anymore."

"You think we won't tell Warby, but we will," Lebo chided, wagging a finger into Harvey's face. "She's the real boss around here, you better know."

"Come on," Jude said, clapping Lebo on the back. "We're just about done."

As Lebo and Jude unloaded the last two casks of liquor off the Damselfly, they heard Monty trundle up the path. He parked the car, and he and Warby both stepped out as the others approached.

"Evening, Warby," Bishop said, letting the clipboard fall to his side.

"Hello, Sidney."

They stood staring at each other in the light of the headlamps for a moment as Monty lowered the trunk door with a grunt.

"King Arthur's court over there," Jude muttered to Harvey. Harvey turned his head with a snort.

"Alright now, let's get her loaded up before we lose any more daylight," Lebo said, clapping his giant hands together.

"Just a minute," Monty spoke up from the back of the car. He came forward toward Bishop. "I got a fishy feeling when we were heading out of town. Nobody out and about. Nobody on the roads either."

"So?" Jude asked, though the suggestion of unease from Monty brought a fluttering in his stomach. "It's getting dark, just like Lebo said."

"It's been like that all day," Warby said, crossing her arms over her chest. She wore an almost comically oversized cardigan over her dress. Jude wondered if it belonged to Bishop. "Nobody running errands, very few folks driving around."

"What does that mean?" Harvey asked, his eyes flicking between each of their faces. "Is that really so strange?"

Bishop drummed his fingers on the back of his clipboard, his lips thin. "Word travels fast in communities like Whitmill. Something may have gotten out that's making folks nervous. Did you hear anything, Warby?"

Warby's hand drifted up to finger her collar. "Not much. A train passed through a few days back and dropped off some men. They were with the sheriff, we thought, but others said they didn't recognize them. It made everyone a little jumpy."

Jude felt Harvey's eyes on him. "Jude—"

"Hush," Jude muttered back. "It ain't nothing."

Bishop fell quiet, his eyes trained on the ground as he thought. "Alright," he said finally. "Monty, we're only going to send half with you tonight. We've got to be able to hide the booze in the car, and we won't be able to do that if it's all loaded. I don't want any trouble in case you get stopped on the road."

Monty nodded. "I think that's wisest."

"What about the rest of it?" Jude asked.

"I can circle back around tonight for it," Monty said.

"No," Bishop interrupted. "It'll be safest back on the Damselfly."

"Now hold on, we can just set up guard here tonight," Lebo protested.

Bishop shook his head. "Our best bet is to have it back on the Damselfly. Lebo, run some circuits, don't stay in one spot longer than an hour or two."

"Hell, Sid, we just unloaded the damn thing. This is a whole lot of trouble just because some folks didn't go to the store for peanuts today."

"This order is critical, Lebo," Bishop said, his voice suddenly loud and sharp. "I'm not taking any chances with it. If we don't deliver this order, we lose more than just the money."

They all fell quiet, everyone staring at Bishop. For a few moments, the only sound was the river lapping against the Damselfly. Jude crossed his arms. He didn't like being left in the blue. He had gotten used to this gig over the past few weeks, and he wasn't so sure he wanted the boat rocked. "Out with it already, Bishop," he said. "Quit talking in circles."

Bishop's eyes flicked over to Jude. Monty and Warby were watching Bishop a little warily, and Jude realized that they must know something about this secret scheme of his, too. Lebo and Harvey were the only ones who looked bewildered. Bishop glanced over at Lebo, clearing his throat with sudden discomfort as he felt the attention on himself.

"Somebody going to clue us in?" Lebo asked, sticking his hands into his pockets.

"I don't—I'm not prepared to say any more until I know things are more certain." Bishop stared at Warby for a moment, and she looked down at her hands. "I've been listening more than you think, Warby. I don't want us to do this forever. But I can't change things without a plan. And the plan needs…money."

Another long pause, this time broken by Monty. "Enough lollygagging," he grunted. "Get the car loaded. I don't want to leave Patsy long tonight."

Jude, Lebo, and Harvey wordlessly entered back into the mill, bringing out bottles and small casks. Monty flicked open a smuggler's hatch below one of the seats, and they tucked other bottles in and around, tossing a few old blankets around to cover the shapes of the casks. Monty climbed back into the car.

"Warby—want me to take you back into town?"

Warby shook her head. "I'm going to stay for a bit."

"Suit yourself," he said. He gave Bishop a sharp look. "Mind you get her home safe."

"Alright, let's get the other half back on the boat," Lebo said, rubbing his eyes with a sigh. "I sure worked up an appetite something fierce."

Jude's stomach had been growling for the past half-hour. "We can get the rest of this," he said, heading back to the storeroom. "Get some grub going."

"I'll help you, Lebo," Warby spoke up. She turned to look at Harvey. "You still mind that arm, you hear?"

"Yes ma'am," Harvey said with a smile.

"Well, if y'all insist." Lebo rubbed his hands together. "I got some potatoes down there, they'll sure taste good once I get them going in a skillet. Miss Warby, you good at peeling spuds?"

Harvey caught up to Jude as Warby and Lebo headed down to the Damselfly.

"Jude," he started in a whisper. Bishop was somewhere behind them. "What's going on?"

"I don't know." Jude lifted a crate with a grunt. "Bishop's

cooking up something, but he won't say much more than what he told y'all just now."

"You've been in on it?"

"Hardly."

Bishop brushed past them, shrugging off his suit jacket and draping it over a wooden chair before taking up a couple casks. Harvey grabbed a jug with his good arm, and they followed Bishop mutely back outside and down to the Damselfly, where they stacked the liquor on the deck. Lebo and Warby's voices drifted up from below deck, Warby laughing quietly as Lebo began singing a ballad of some sort. They continued to make trips back and forth as they emptied the storeroom.

Jude followed Harvey back up the knoll, leaving Bishop starting to organize the jugs and casks on the deck. They were nearly up to the mill again when Jude saw a slight jerk in Harvey's neck. He thought nothing of it, re-emerging into the mill and heading back to the storeroom. Harvey hooked him by the shirt collar and pushed him back toward the wall by the mill door.

"What the hell!"

"Look, look," Harvey whispered.

Jude glanced out of the open doorway, and he saw a figure shift by the trees nearby. A second was crouched in the bushes by the mouth of the road.

Jude cursed below his breath. "I'll be damned. You've been looking out after all."

"It's Teague, isn't it?"

"That's my guess." Jude's mind jumped to a dozen different places at once. Where were the guns? How many doors did the mill have? How many men were closing in?

"Shit. We gotta get Bishop."

"No," Jude said, stilling Harvey with his hand. "They haven't moved in yet, we'll just tip them off if they see us running for Bishop. Come on, there's guns somewhere in the back."

"What about Lebo and Warby?" Harvey whispered as they ran to another back room in the mill.

"Lebo's got a couple pistols in the boat, he can manage," Jude said. It was hard to see in the room. "Grab that lantern out there, Harv. Quick."

Harvey jogged back with the lantern, and they could see a row of firearms laid out on a big wooden table. Jude grabbed a revolver, checking the cartridge—full—before handing it to Harvey.

"You good with this?"

"Yeah, yeah. Hurry up."

Jude grabbed a shotgun and stuck another revolver into his belt, shoving extra shells into his back pocket. He spotted a coil of braided cord and slung it over his shoulders. "Alright. Back door," he said.

"What's the plan?"

"They're spread out, probably gonna try and rush us once Bishop gets back up here. We may be able to pick a few off in the back first—don't shoot unless you have to." They were by the back door now, and Jude reached out to open it. He paused, turning to look back at Harvey.

"Harv. You got my back?"

Harvey gave him a nod. His face was flushed, but his eyes were alert. "I've got your back."

Chapter Eighteen

"I don't see anyone," Jude whispered. "I'll break left, you go right."

"Okay. Go."

Jude ran in a half-crouch to the left, staying close to the side of the mill. He wished for summertime crickets and the scream of cicadas, but instead the only sounds to mask his footfalls were the current of the river and a wind, which whistled faintly since there were no leaves to rustle on the trees. He came on the corner of the building and peered cautiously over. His heart stuttered in his chest as he saw him, a man crouching behind an outcrop of mountain laurels, facing the other direction.

It was mostly dark now, the blooming colors of sunset quickly succumbing to purple and indigo in the sky. Jude didn't have much faith in his ability to creep up behind the man, not with the thick layers of brittle underbrush on the woodland edge. He would just have to come as close as he could, then rush him.

Jude inched forward, trying to breathe slowly and evenly through his nose. He was close enough now to hear the man spit out a stream of tobacco from the side of his mouth. Jude waited for a minute or two, and as the man made a faint snorting sound, gathering the saliva in his mouth, Jude rushed forward, delivering a quick strike to the man's skull with the butt of his shotgun. It wasn't enough to knock him out—he tumbled to the side with a dazed grunt, dropping his gun. Jude acted quickly, plucking a bandana out of his pocket and shoving it into the man's mouth before rolling him over and tying his hands and legs together with the cord he had grabbed. He cut the cord with his pocketknife and swept the area with his eyes, wondering if anyone had heard their brief scuffle. No other sounds—he hoped that boded well for Harvey.

The man groaned again, laying on his side in the underbrush. Jude grabbed the man's rifle and slunk toward the front of the mill, keeping low. He dropped the rifle in one of the bushes, pushing a few dead leaves over it. The two men he had spied near the front of the mill must have moved closer in. Jude saw one more figure hovering at the front corner of the mill, serving as lookout.

A branch snapped under Jude's foot, and the figure turned. It was a kid, no older than thirteen or fourteen. His gun looked heavy in his hands. Jude snapped his own shotgun up, hissing, "Drop it."

Shock, then fury passed over the boy's face. He lowered his rifle, but didn't release it.

"Drop it, kid," Jude repeated, moving in closer. The kid didn't even have stubble on his face. Was Teague really willing to bring along a child to a vengeance raid? Jude jerked the rifle out of the boy's hands in disgust. He nudged the boy forward with the barrel of his shotgun, moving his finger off the trigger once the boy's back was to him.

"How many are there?"

"Go to hell," the boy spat.

Jude could hear voices inside the mill now. A quick glance down at the Damselfly confirmed that Bishop was no longer there. Warm yellow light spilled out of the portholes of the boat, broken every now and then as Warby or Lebo moved within. All was well there, at least. Jude guessed all of the other thugs had rushed into the mill once Bishop had entered.

"Jude," Harvey whispered. He was crouched near the opposite corner of the mill. He gestured toward the doorway with the revolver in his hand. "The rest of them are in there. Teague and three others."

"You sure that's all of them?"

"Yeah. Knocked two others over the head on this side. I've been looking for a little bit, I don't see no one else."

Jude saw the boy's ribcage expand, and he clapped his hand over the boy's mouth just as he was about to shout out. "Shut it," he snapped into the boy's ear.

"Jesus, he's just a kid," Harvey whispered as he came up alongside Jude by the door.

Veins stood out on the boy's neck and temples, his face turning red with fury. *You're just a pawn, kid,* Jude thought. Through the door, they could hear meaty thuds followed by sharp grunts of pain.

"Come on," Jude said, jerking his head toward the door. "Bishop's in hot water."

"What's the plan?"

Jude glanced at the back of the boy's head. "Just follow my lead."

They crept quietly inside the mill, spotting Teague and three of his men in the middle of the cavernous main room, by the old grist stone. Two of the men were holding Bishop by the arms, while another shook his fist out from a punch. Bishop's head hung low on his chest, his once-immaculate shirt already speckled with blood.

They could hear Teague speaking: "...got yourself a pretty cushy order in, I hear. I'm impressed, Bishop. If I could have nicked the whole thing from you, I might have considered it payment for that showdown at Andersons' the other week. But, seeing as how only half the order's here—" He nodded to the man in front of Bishop, who wound up his arm and drove another punch into Bishop's gut. Bishop doubled over, letting out a growled gasp.

Jude stepped forward into the light of the lanterns, the shotgun trained on the boy's back. "I'd step down about now, boys, if I were you," he called out. Harvey moved alongside him, his revolver poised.

Teague turned, his face slackening at the sight of the boy. He held a shotgun in his hand, but the other men had their pistols in their belts. They made to grab for them, but Harvey broke off to the side.

"Hands up," he commanded sharply. The revolver held steady in his hand.

Slowly, the men raised their hands. Bishop collapsed to the ground, coughing. Teague's face had turned dark with rage, and he held onto his shotgun.

"You heard the man," Jude said. "Drop it, Teague."

"Donny, you hurt?" Teague snapped.

Jude grabbed the boy by the shoulder, pressing the barrel of the shotgun against his head. "You want him to be?" Jude kept his eyes locked with Teague. "I said drop the damn gun."

Teague's shotgun clattered to the ground. "Let him go. Come on, he's just—"

"Just a kid?" Jude walked slowly forward. Harvey stayed trained on the other three. "What did you think would happen if you brought a kid to something like this? Piece of shit, that's what you are."

"You all right, Bishop?" Harvey asked.

Bishop rose up to one knee, turning his head to one side and spitting out a spray of blood. "There are others outside," he murmured hoarsely.

"We took care of them."

"Y'all meddling in business you ain't ought to meddle in," Teague growled. "This is a score between me and Bishop."

"We tried to tell you he'd come back, Sid," Jude said.

Bishop snapped out a handkerchief to wipe his mouth, glaring at Jude with one blackened eye.

"What now, Bishop?" Harvey asked. His eyes flicked for the barest second over to Jude. Jude could read that expression—he was wondering, same as Jude was, if they would have to kill each of these men. Jude's stomach already squirmed just holding the gun against the boy's head.

"You came here to kill me tonight, Teague," Bishop said, his voice low. He rose slowly to his feet, coming to stand in front of Teague. Teague met his eye, chin thrust upward.

Jude thought quickly, memories of the mine camps and bands of unionizers returning to his mind. He thought of the Baldwin-Felts beating some of the workers to a pulp, ransacking their cabins, shooting others who fought back, all to send a message to the rest of the miners: Unions not tolerated. Oftentimes, though, the overseers had them evict entire families from their homes, banishing them from the camp entirely. This was the graver punishment for most of the miners, robbed of livelihood, shelter, and community all at once. Shooting made martyrs, but banishment broke their spirits.

Jude shoved the boy roughly forward with the shotgun barrel, and he stumbled forward to rush beside Teague. Bishop's head snapped up, his eyes very sharp. Harvey glanced at him a few times, still watching the other three men. Jude pulled the other revolver out of his belt, sliding it across the floor toward Bishop, who picked it up. He watched Jude warily, but said nothing.

"Here's the thing Bishop doesn't understand, Mr. Teague," Jude began. His finger was on the trigger now. "If we let you and your boys go, you'll just come back another day to kill him."

Teague had his arm out slightly in front of his son, watching Jude with hard, glittering eyes.

"But," Jude continued, "if we kill you, someone else in your gang's just going to hop back up and take your place, won't they? Could be that kid beside you," Jude gestured with his shotgun, "could be a brother, doesn't matter. They'll be out for blood. That's what Bishop doesn't understand, alright. He doesn't keep scores. He was the one who let you go at the lumber mill, all because you were in retreat."

Teague snorted. "Like hell. He shot me, is what he did."

"He didn't, I did." Jude saw Harvey glance at him sharply out of the corner of his eye. In case something went awry, he didn't want Teague or any of his men coming later to hunt down Harvey. But he wouldn't have to worry about that, if he pulled this off. "I was a little off my mark that day."

Veins stood out on Teague's forehead, his mouth pulled into a hard line.

"Here's what we're going to do, then," Jude said. "You're going to take your family and all your cronies, and you're going to leave Whitmill. Actually, you're going to leave the county. The whole damn county. And if you so much as inch one toe over the county line, we'll shoot you. Not just you, but your boys, even that beanpole kid beside you." Jude kept his eyes on Teague, not looking at the kid, not looking at Bishop or Harvey. If he looked away, they'd see through him.

Teague sneered at him. "You really think you can make us do that?"

Jude cocked the shotgun, thrusting the barrel under Teague's chin. "You listen here, you belly-crawling son of a bitch." He spoke fast and low, where he doubted Bishop or the others could hear him. "I became a Baldwin-Felts agent at seventeen. I've shot countless men, killed others, pulled women and children screaming from their houses, watched as those homes were burned before their very eyes. I've lead raids with ex-convicts who'd done things that would make your toes curl. They all answered to me, they did what I said—you hear what I'm saying? I can make you do anything I want, and if you don't, just you see if I don't raze your people to the ground."

The whites of Teague's eyes were glowing. The boy, Donny, was frozen behind him, his face ashen.

"Pa," he croaked. "Come on, let's go. Let's go, Pa."

Teague began to shuffle backwards, grabbing hold of his son's arm. The other three men followed him, hands still in the air, Bishop and Harvey staying trained on them.

"Bishop, Harvey, go outside and get the others out there,"

Jude said, keeping his eyes locked on Teague. He pushed them slowly back out the mill door, and Bishop and Harvey appeared a moment later, pushing forward the other three men, who stumbled groggily from their head wounds.

"Baldwin-Felts."

Jude's eyes swiveled back to Teague. "That's what I said."

Teague half-turned his head, the faintest smile on his weathered face. "I know someone who's looking for you."

Jude didn't turn to see if Harvey could hear. Out loud, he said, "Bishop, Harvey, get down to the boat and make sure the others are alright. I can take care of this."

He heard Bishop and Harvey gradually break away and head back toward the boat.

"Who's looking for me?" Jude asked when they were out of earshot.

A ripple of humorless laughter rolled out of Teague. "You'll get what's coming to you. You mark my words."

Chapter Nineteen

Teague's men were far up the road now. They had broken into a run as soon as they reached a bend in the road, and Jude let them scramble. He walked backwards, slowly, for a few minutes until he could no longer hear their retreating footsteps. His breath rose in clouds as he turned back toward the mill. He could see the Damselfly bobbing on the river below, the world murky and dark contrasted against the rosy glow of the boat.

Jude shambled down toward the river, his nerves raw and his mind disturbed. He had not liked Teague's hinting words. They needed to pull away from the mill, keep moving like Bishop had first said. And he and Harvey needed to be on twice the lookout if Teague meant what he thought he did.

The lapping of the water against the Damselfly usually soothed him—Jude had slept better aboard the Damselfly over the past few weeks than he had ever slept in his life—but now the sound seemed rough and loud. Jude hauled himself heavily aboard.

"Bishop, Harvey, it's me," Jude said as he opened the door below deck. It was quiet in the cabin, and Jude thought he heard a muffled moan. The hair stood up on the back of his neck. He paused on the stairs before moving slowly down.

"Harvey," he said again. "Bishop."

The first thing he saw was Warby and Harvey, sitting against a wall with gags in their mouths. Warby's eyes were streaming with tears, and Harvey had a dark red bruise developing over the left side of his face. Warby let out a hoarse whimper, straining her shoulders—her hands seemed to be tied behind her back. Bishop was slumped near the bottom of the stairs, out cold. Harvey looked barely conscious, but he was staring at the opposite side of the cabin.

"Harv—" Jude started, following his gaze. He saw Lebo slouched in the corner, his chin resting on his chest. Jude knelt beside him, only to stumble back a moment later. There was a gaping bloody hole in Lebo's stomach. He was dead.

Warby let out an urgent squeal through her gag, and Jude whirled around to see a fifth figure behind him, closing the cabin door. There was that pungent, rancid smell.

"Didn't that work a treat?" Prince's voice floated down the steps. Harvey's bleary eyes glided over to watch as Prince descended into the cabin with them. He had a rifle in his hands. "Didn't think we'd have this extra crowd, though," Prince said. "You know, I came down here because I thought the boat would make a tidy little escape, if the need came up. Little did I know your pal there was cooking away, along with this little mountain flower—" Prince leered at Warby.

"Shut your mouth," Jude said.

Prince laughed and waved his rifle toward Jude. "I don't think I will, Washer. You see, I've followed you and Morgan all the way from Virginia, and I think I deserve to enjoy this moment, don't you?"

Jude rose to his feet slowly, keeping an eye on Prince's rifle. "What do you want?"

Prince ran his tongue over his lips. His eyes drifted over to Warby. "I want quite a few things, Washer. Care to hear my wish list?"

"What do you want?" Jude repeated, hands tightening into fists by his side.

"With you?" Prince let out a sigh, rubbing his free hand over his chin. "Well, after that gag you pulled at the mine raid, Bradshaw put a price on you and Morgan's heads. And I wasn't about to let someone else get to you first. A couple other Baldwins followed me down here and got close to finding you, too. But we took care of them, didn't we, sweetheart?" Prince lifted up his rifle and kissed the barrel.

"You saw us on the train. Didn't you?"

"If you mean did I see your ugly face, no, I didn't. But I saw blood on the edge of the cart, and I took a hint that you'd hopped the train. Pretty damn impressive, considering Morgan still had my bullet in him. How the hell did you manage that?" Prince's canine teeth flashed as he laughed. "I sure couldn't figure it out, but I grabbed a car and made my way down to every station stop until I got down here. Found the train getting loaded for the next track, and your cart was empty." Prince tapped the side of his nose. "But I picked up the scent after smelling all that spilled moonshine. Got a little mixed up though, found Teague first. He ain't exactly shy about his business, neither. He liked putting a new face to work, got me scouting out his competition. And, what do you know, look who I found."

"If you want us for Bradshaw's bounty, then get us out of here." Jude gestured to Lebo's body, unwilling to take another look. "There was no need—no need for this."

"Like his life was worth horse shit," Prince said with a laugh. "Come on Jude, you've shot dozens of coots just like him in the raids. Little late to get all high and mighty."

Jude tried to catch Harvey's eyes, but the boy was staring at Lebo. His eyes were bleary, his head drooping slightly over his chest. How hard had Prince hit him? Hate seethed beneath Jude's skin, the adrenaline beginning to resurge.

"You know, Jude," Prince continued, "Bradshaw filled me in on some of your family history before I left Bluefield. Seems turning your back on people is sort of your specialty, huh?"

Prince ambled across the room, his rifle held lazily by his side. He crouched beside Warby, who watched him with the whites of her eyes gleaming. "You see, pumpkin, Jude Washer here turned over his own daddy to us Baldwin boys and had him killed, all before he could even grow a hair on his chin."

"That's a lie," Jude said. "I didn't have him killed."

"Oh didn't you?" Prince asked. "Because you sure did turn him over, and his name sure was on that roster Bradshaw gave me."

Jude's stomach turned to lead. "What roster?"

Prince clucked. "Aw, Jude baby, don't tell me you never even bothered to see if he was on the dead list?" Prince hooked his finger under Warby's jaw, thrusting her face up to his. "See, he's got no shame at all. Got his own daddy killed, and didn't even bother—"

"Don't touch her," Jude barked.

Prince's eyes flicked up to Jude, the smirk fading from his mouth. "You know, I'm getting pretty tired of you telling me what to do. If you haven't noticed, you're not with the Baldwin-Felts anymore. You aren't calling the shots. I am. And I've decided that Morgan's bounty will be more than enough to fill my wallet. But you—" Prince rose to his feet, crossing the room and thrusting the rifle under Jude's chin. Jude froze, a wave of vertigo washing over him.

"I think I've decided," Prince whispered, so that only Jude could hear, "that's it's time to give the traitor a traitor's end."

They left Harvey and Warby with their hands and ankles bound, and a gag in their mouths. Bishop had not stirred. Jude hoped he was passed out, and not worse. He hadn't been able to check.

Prince led Jude away with the rifle at his back, grabbing a loop of rope above deck before they left the Damselfly. Prince nudged Jude forward with the rifle, into the dense trees past the mill. Jude watched the mill as they moved farther and farther away, his brain numbly remembering the control he had felt mere minutes before, holding Teague and his men at gunpoint. Now he had Prince's gun pressed against his spine, pushing him deeper into the woods.

"Well I'll be damned," Prince said from behind him. He started laughing.

"What?" Jude snapped.

"Look yonder, Jude, and tell me what tree you see there."

It was almost pitch black in the woods, and Jude had already tripped over several lower shrubs and logs. "What tree? How the hell can you see anything out here?"

"Some of us are used to being out in the dark," Prince drawled. He shoved Jude and he stumbled forward, catching hold of a slender tree trunk to balance himself. "This one," Prince said.

Jude looked up at the tree he held onto. He could see very little in the dim starlight that filtered through the tree branches. But now he recognized the tree, not from its shape but by the small blossoms that covered its limbs. It was a redbud tree, one of the only trees to bloom so early in the spring, when the other trees hadn't even put on leaf.

"They say Judas Iscariot hung himself on a redbud tree after betraying Jesus," Prince said. His voice seemed immense and unattached in the long expanse of forest. It was silent, no insects or crunching leaves or wind. The mill was no longer visible, and Jude couldn't hear the river anymore. "Some folks still call them Judas trees. You ever heard that before?"

Jude had heard it before—it was a common wives' tale in the mountains, but instead he said, "Sounds like a shit story you just made up."

Prince laughed. "Maybe, maybe not. But either way, you're going to meet your end the same way." His voice was right by Jude's ear, and Jude felt the rope drop over his neck and tighten.

Jude's gasp was cut short as his trachea flattened. He clawed at the rope and was able to relieve the pressure for a bare second before Prince pulled tighter, cackling like a hyena.

"Tell me, Jude," Prince panted, "is it true you've got a dead brother? Did you kill him? Or did you let someone else do that for you, too?"

Fury and panic warred inside Jude. He struggled against the rope, which Prince seemed to be pulling at with all his weight. Jude could feel his strength weakening as his lungs failed to fill with air.

"Bradshaw said," Prince grunted, tugging the rope tighter—Jude could feel him forming a knot—"that you hated your daddy because he killed your brother. That true, Jude?"

The pressure released abruptly, and Jude could feel his lungs unfurl like sails as he took in gulps of air. A moment later, though, and Jude felt Prince slide the knot up against the nape of his neck.

"Couldn't kill Daddy yourself, Jude? Had to get someone else to do your dirty work? God, you're pathetic. You've never stood up and fought in your life."

Jude opened his mouth, his throat aching. All that came out when he tried to speak was a strangled howl, and he leapt forward and threw Prince to the ground. The noose was still around Jude's neck, and Prince tried to grab the rope again. Jude pinned down his arm and pounded him in the face as hard as his shaking limbs would allow. Prince grunted in pain, momentarily stunned, but a second later returned with a punch to Jude's ribs. Jude lost his balance, tumbling off Prince and feeling his back hit the cold leaf litter on the ground. Prince scrambled up with a grunt and stood over Jude, lifting his foot and stomping down. Jude rolled to the side just in time, Prince's foot landing where Jude's face had been a moment before.

Up on his knees, Jude tackled Prince's legs and pushed him into the ground. For a moment it was a scramble between them to gain the upper hand. It hurt Jude to move his neck, to breathe, to let out the sounds of rage that rose in his throat like feral growls. Prince, too, was panting with the effort to fend Jude off, and the smell and sound of him filled Jude with repulsion. The white flash of Prince's eyes triggered an instinct in Jude; it drowned out all other thought and replaced it with white-hot fury. Jude pinned Prince down and landed his first strike, the strength surging back into his arms, and blood appeared on Prince's face. Jude did not stop. He beat him again and again, his fist hammering an invisible nail into Prince's skull.

"He was my brother," Jude shouted, his voice coming out hoarse and echoing through the trees. He had Prince by the shoulders now, lifting him up and slamming him into the frozen ground below. "Don't you dare—say—I killed him. I didn't kill—I didn't kill him—I didn't—"

Prince didn't struggle against him anymore. Jude still struck him with a rhythmic pounding, his own face wet, with blood or tears or mucus, he wasn't sure.

"Jude!" a voice shouted. It was loud, but at the same time seemed miles away to Jude. He felt a pair of hands close around his shoulder and he struck out blindly behind him. A second later and he felt himself being tugged off Prince.

"Leave me be!" Jude yelled, flailing at the body behind him.

"Stop, Jude, he's gone—"

Jude struggled wildly with a yell. He wanted to keep pounding his fist into that face, that hateful face, until it was deep in the ground, where he would never see it again. If he could bury it, just bury it, he would never have to think about it again.

The body behind him grunted with the effort of restraint. "Jude, it's me. It's me!" An arm crossed like an iron bar over Jude's chest, holding him back.

The strength ebbed from Jude's limbs. He went limp, sagging back onto his knees. "Willis," he croaked. "I'm sorry, Willis—"

"Jude, it's me. It's—"

"I should have fought him, I should have taken care of you— I'm sorry—I'm sorry—"

Jude doubled over, his entire body heaving with shuddering breaths. The arm slid back from his chest until he felt the hands move to grip his shoulders.

"It's over now, Jude. I've got your back."

Chapter Twenty

Jude cradled a cup of coffee in his hands, staring at the wood grain of Warby's kitchen table. Bishop, Monty, Warby, and Harvey sat around the table as well, nobody willing to break the silence. Less than an hour had passed since Lebo's burial. Bishop had a preacher from somewhere in the hills come and perform a graveside service. Several people had crowded around the grave, Jude recognizing some of them as moonshiners. They didn't ask any questions.

"I should have acted sooner," Bishop said finally. He looked terrible—the swelling around his eye had gone down, but it was gruesomely bruised. "Lebo warned me there would be no end to the fighting. I didn't act soon enough."

Jude's eyes traced the whorls of the woodgrain that formed

a knot in the table. "Lebo died because I led a Baldwin down here."

"Weren't your fault, Jude," Monty murmured. "If that bastard hadn't done it, Teague would have eventually, and the rest of us too. Baldwin or bootlegger, they're all the same type. Out for themselves and no one else."

Jude took a long drink of coffee. It was bitter, and too hot in his mouth.

"What now?" Harvey asked.

Jude struggled to look at Harvey. He had a gruesome bruise across his eye and cheekbone, but worse than that was remembering how Harvey had found him in the woods: next to Prince's dead body—beaten to a pulp—and Jude babbling like a broken child.

Bishop cleared his throat, shifting in his chair. "Perhaps it's uncouth to make a business proposition at this time. But I believe it would serve to fulfill Lebo's ultimate wish."

They all looked up at Bishop, hands gripping mugs of coffee.

"Ready to show you cards now, huh?" Jude asked.

Bishop took a deep breath. "We've run this hooch business for close to ten years now. I've stuck with it because—well, because I thought it was the only way to make money up here. And, I don't think I was wrong. There's no jobs up here, for us or the others." Bishop turned to look them each in the eye. "Lebo was right all along. These people are poor and proud, and unwilling to leave their land. It's all they have. I thought we were helping them by running their hooch, but I was wrong. If we want to help these people—help ourselves—we've got to give up running hooch."

"How do you suggest we all make a living, then?" Monty asked, leaning back in his chair and crossing his arms.

Bishop reached over the table and grasped Warby's hand,

exchanging a look with her before turning back to the rest of them. "If you're willing to listen to a risky plan, then I believe I have a solution."

"Riskier than bootlegging?" Harvey asked.

A faint smirk crossed Bishop's face. "In a way. It's going to take a lot of work, if we're to pull it off. I'd like to propose we convert the mill back to its original purpose." Monty snorted, but Bishop raised a finger before he could protest. "Not a gristmill. A textile mill."

"Textiles?" Jude asked, brow furrowing.

"There are farmers not forty miles away growing cotton," Warby spoke up. "Right now they sell their crops mostly to mills in Gastonia. There are dozens of textile mills there, and they've created hundreds of jobs. We could do that here."

Jude rose his hand, shaking his head. "Look, this is a pretty idea, but those mills aren't so different from the coal mines. They build their mill villages and pay the workers in scrip, just like the miners. They're having more and more strikes, too," Jude added, exchanging glances with Harvey.

"We would mandate that all laborers are paid in cash currency, not scrip. And we don't have the funds to build a mill village, not yet anyway. The people would get to stay in their own homes. Now, I'm not saying we'd be making any millionaires—"

"Bishop," Monty began with a sigh, "do you have any idea how much money it would take to make this happen?"

"I do. And—" Bishop took in a deep breath, leaning forward on the table, "after the money we got from that order, we're not so far away from having what we need."

"You've got to be joking," Jude scoffed. "Enough money for—"

"Equipment, raw materials, and a salary for a foreman I'm

going to hire from a mill in Gastonia. He knows how to run the machines and can instruct the workers. We already own the mill building, so that's taken care of."

"And money to pay the workers?" Harvey prompted. "Is there enough for that?"

"There will be, for the first few months," Bishop answered. He paused. "If we sell the Damselfly."

They all fell silent. Jude thought of the Damselfly and the weeks of boating quietly up and down the river, eating meals and playing cards below deck, humming songs in the bunkbeds before sleep—those memories were now disrupted by the image of Lebo's bloodied body slumped in the kitchen corner. It could no longer be home for them.

"You're right, it's a harebrained idea," Monty said, at last breaking the silence. "But Lebo would have been all for it."

Warby blinked rapidly, nodding. Jude cleared his throat. "What do you need from us?"

Bishop laughed grimly. "I'll know more once I get the fore-man down here. We'll need shift supervisors, and he can train us to understand the machines and facilitate the workers. But that will come in time. Right now, we need to recruit workers. Now, there's plenty of the moonshiners who I know will accept in a heartbeat. Some of them, though—well, they're not likely to see change as friendly, even if it means getting them out of moonshining. They've never trusted me to begin with, I was too much of an outsider. That's why I always let Lebo do the talking." Bishop turned to Jude. "That's where I could use you. You may be a stranger, but you're more like these people than I am. They'll accept you quicker than they ever did me."

"We'll need a base crew to get going, and hope that others start to join later," Warby added.

"I can make our normal route and talk to folks, see who's interested," Monty volunteered.

Bishop nodded. "That's a good start. Jude, Harvey—any chance you know anyone besides Baldwin-Felts?"

Jude and Harvey exchanged glances. "Your family?" Jude suggested.

Harvey nodded slowly. "I'll have to write to them. They'll be hard pressed to leave the farm—but I could maybe convince them."

"What about you?" Bishop asked Jude.

Jude looked back down at his mug of coffee. "I don't have any family."

"Nobody else you think would want in?" Warby asked quietly.

An idea grew slowly in his mind. "I might have someone who could be interested. If I can find them."

"We can spare you for a while, if that's what it takes," Bishop said. He raised an eyebrow. "As long as you promise to come back."

Jude smiled grimly. It would be easy to head into the woods and disappear, leave behind Harvey and the others to clean up the mess in this corner of the mountains. Part of him felt surprised that he didn't want to leave. The thought of just getting up from this kitchen table where they were all clustered was disagreeable to him.

He wanted to stay here, drink another cup of coffee, maybe find a guitar and pick out the chords of "Shady Grove." He wanted to carve a set of wood chimes for Warby to hang on her front porch. He wanted to play a round of poker with Harvey and Monty and Bishop, and teach Harvey how to make a decent bluff for once. He wanted to see cotton turned into thread, and thread turned into fabric, and fabric turned into money. He wanted to find a little place by the river, it could be a shed for all he cared, and he wanted to just listen to rain tapping on the surface of the water.

He'd come back.

Epilogue

Jude dipped his hands into the mountain stream, splashing water onto his face to clear away the remaining bristles of the beard he had just shaven off. It had taken him a week to make his way up through the mountains and arrive back in Virginia, and a few days more to track down the right mine camp. In that time it seemed as though spring had arrived overnight, and the canopy of trees overhead were growing leaves like fine green feathers. Wild daffodils spangled the forest floor like sunshine filtering through the tree boughs, and the redbud trees had been surpassed by white dogwoods.

The day before, Jude had spoken with the mine foreman and confirmed which house he needed to go to. His stomach roiled with anxiety he had not felt before. It was different from the dread he used to feel before a raid. The tightness in his chest and the race of his heartbeat had as much to do with hope as it did fear.

Jude tried to survey the sliver of his own reflection he could see in the blade of his razor. He had achieved a good shave, and even though his hair was wet, at least it no longer reeked of sweat from days of walking. Jude could not do much about the condition of his clothes, so he was as tidy as he was able to make himself. He tucked his razor and shaving brush back into his bag and made his way out of the woods. The mine camp was only a short walk away.

Same as yesterday, when Jude had first entered the camp, his stomach clenched at the sight of the ramshackle huts and the acrid smell of coal that seemed to cling to everything in the camp. He followed the foreman's instructions as close as he could, eventually coming upon a pitiful cabin near the edge of the camp. The logs were sloppily fit together, with several visible gaps and a poor foundation. A girl was stringing sheets upon a clothesline, frowning as the wind tried to whip the sheets out of her grasp. Jude let himself watch her for a few moments from afar, studying her face and feeling a painful ache in his chest.

After a minute Jude strode forward. He did not want to walk up too fast and put her on guard, but neither did he want to startle her by approaching too quietly. She did not notice him until he was only a few steps away, her eyes flicking up absently, but then focusing back on his face as her hands paused on the clothesline. Recognition sparked in her eyes.

"Hello Florrie," Jude said, slipping his hat off his head.

Her mouth formed words that didn't come out. She glanced

behind her, then back at Jude. "How did you know to find us here?" she finally asked. She stood with her body diagonal to him—ready to run.

"I don't mean to scare you," Jude said. He rotated the brim of his hat in his hands. "I recognized you too, last time. I—you know who I am, don't you?"

Florrie faced him, no longer looking like she was about to bound off like a startled doe. She had her mother's broad cheekbones, and her mouth was set in a straight, defiant line. "I know you, Jude Washer," she said. Jude heard the Irish in her voice. A smile broke out on his face at hearing his name spoken in that accent.

"I know you've got every reason not to trust me," Jude said, taking a slow step forward. Florrie did not back away, but watched him. He expected to see hate in her eyes, but could only see wariness and confusion. She was still so young, too young to have been through what she had already. "I'm here to see your ma, if she's here."

Florrie looked back at the cabin, then turned back to Jude. "We've just moved in here," she said. "Da had to find new work," she added with coldness.

"I know," Jude said. "I've come to try and get you all out of this. We're starting a mill down—"

"Florrie," called a voice from the cabin. Jude's throat tightened. "Surely you're done with the laundry, my girl?"

Mam Myers stepped out of the cabin, brushing flour from her hands. She was stouter and had streaks of gray in her hair, but it was undoubtedly Mam Myers. Jude could feel a tremor in his hands, and he gripped his hat tighter.

Mam Myers glanced at Flossie and Jude. "Yes sir?" she asked.

"If you're here for the deposit, I told the foreman already we'd have it in next Tuesday."

Jude stepped forward, unable to break his eyes away from her face. He moistened his lips, finding his mouth suddenly dry. "Mam Myers," he said. "I've—I've come to make things right."

Mam Myers raised a shaking hand to her mouth. "Oh, lamb."

Acknowledgments

You're holding this book because a whole bunch of people came alongside me, built me up, and worked hard to make this happen.

Mama, thank you for reading to us every morning and making me keep a journal as a kid—that's what really got me started. Daddy, your stories every night are what made me want to create my own.

Savannah, you were my earliest beta reader, editor, and hype woman. You've always made me feel like the best storyteller in the world. One day, we'll stop daydreaming and actually make one of those creative projects happen together. Seriously. Please?

Benjamin, I would never have had the guts to submit this story for publishing at all without you. You have listened to every apprehension and insecurity and built me back up every time. There's a specific reason I dedicated this book to you—ask me about it later. I love you.

Carrie Stephens, fellow author (*The Zenia Wood*) and trusted writing friend—your insightful feedback on my revisions is what kept me motivated to write (and rewrite). You have encouraged me every step of the way.

Without Dr. Teresa Jones and my senior seminar with her at Anderson University, this book would never have gotten off the ground. Dr. Jones, thank you for your coaching, encouragement, and the confidence you poured into me.

Dr. Randall Wilhelm, it's thanks to your Appalachian Literature class that I first heard about the Baldwin Felts at all. Your office door was always open when I had additional questions, and you never hesitated to lend your own books and resources.

Kate McMullen and the fine folks at Hub City Press—y'all are just the best. Really and truly, I can't imagine a warmer, more supportive introduction into the publishing world.

To every friend, family member, coworker, or passing stranger who has celebrated with me, spread the word, bought the book, written a kind review—thank you, thank you, thank you. I've deserved no part of this amazing experience, so at the end of the day the biggest thanks goes to God and His generosity.

PUBLISHING
New & Extraordinary
VOICES FROM THE
AMERICAN SOUTH

HUB CITY PRESS is a non-profit independent press in Spartanburg, SC that publishes well-crafted, high-quality works by new and established authors, with an emphasis on the Southern experience. We are committed to high-caliber novels, short stories, poetry, plays, memoir, and works emphasizing regional culture and history. We are particularly interested in books with a strong sense of place.

Hub City Press is an imprint of the non-profit Hub City Writers Project, founded in 1995 to foster a sense of community through the literary arts. Our metaphor of organization purposely looks backward to the nineteenth century when Spartanburg was known as the "hub city," a place where railroads converged and departed.

The South Carolina Novel Prize is open to all writers in South Carolina. It is co-sponsored by the South Carolina Arts Commission, the College of Charleston, the South Carolina State Library, and South Carolina Humanities.

PREVIOUS WINNERS

2019: Scott Sharpe *A Wild Eden*

2017: Brock Adams *Ember*

2015: James McTeer *Minnow*

2013: Susan Tekulve *In the Garden of Stone*

2011: Matt Matthews *Mercy Creek*

2009: Brian Ray *Through the Pale Door*

Sabon MT Pro
10.8 / 15.3

9 781938 235849